IT'S GIVIN' RICH THUG ENERGY 2

KEVINA HOPKINS

D1713932

It's Givin' Rich Thug Energy 2

Copyright © 2023 by Kevina Hopkins

All rights reserved.

Published in the United States of America.

Published by Cole Hart Signature, LLC.

Mailing List

To stay up to date on new releases, plus get information on contests, sneak peeks, and more,

Go To The Website Below...

www.colehartsignature.com

PREVIOUSLY ON IT'S GIVIN' RICH THUG ENERGY....

KHALIL

Today has been one hell of a day. I've been so busy that I still haven't talked to Bri yet. The meetings I had went great. I'm about to start seeing more money a month than I've ever seen for my car washes. I was supposed to go to Bri's house after that, but then some shit went down at one of my traps that I needed to handle. On top of that, my pops called and said he needed us to meet up with him. I don't know what the hell is going on. It's like I'm not meant to talk to Bri today or something.

Krystal's ass has been calling me all day since I dropped her off. It got to the point where I had to block her ass. Going to see her yesterday was the dumbest shit I could have ever done, and I'm paying for it now. She was right when she said I should have just let her be, because now she's acting like I hit her crazy button.

I looked down at my watch and realized Joe was almost thirty minutes late. I don't know what's going on with him, but my father is pissed and so am I. I got other shit to do besides sitting here at my parents' crib.

"Where is your brother?" my father asked just as Joe came walking through the house looking pissed.

"Nice of you to join us," I told him.

"Where were you? You're late," my father yelled.

"I'm sorry Pops, I got caught up in some shit because of KB."

"What you mean because of me? What happened?" I asked, not knowing what's going on.

"What happened is you a dumb ass nigga. You went and spent the night with Krystal last night. She called Jayde and told her everything. Jayde's messy ass told Bri, not knowing that she didn't already know. Bri had been at the hospital all day because she got drugged last night. That's why she was acting the way she did. I told you something had to be off because Bri wasn't that kind of girl. Your ass was too busy on some get-back shit with Krystal while your girl was going through hell. I tried to talk to her but she didn't want to. She did give me your key back and said to tell you not to come to her house because she's not answering for you. Oh, and Bri's sister Stacey beat the hell out Jayde because she thinks she might have had something to do with what happened to Bri because those were her friends."

Listening to Joe had me furious. I can't believe a mother-fucker drugged Bri. I feel dumb as shit and wish I could turn back time. As Bri's man, I'm supposed to protect her. I'm supposed to be the one person there when she needs me. I don't know why I would ever think she would consciously cheat on me. Then I ignored her calls while she was at the hospital. She had to go there without me. Now she probably thinks she can't count on me and she'll probably never trust me again.

I don't know how to fix this shit, but I have to figure out a way. It was crazy of me to think that Krystal would keep her mouth closed when she's hurt. I know that she's a vindictive person, but she's never been that way with me. I never thought that I would end up in this kind of situation. I've cheated on Krystal and she always looked the other way. I guess in this situation it's not just about the cheating. It's the circumstances of what caused me to cheat.

"Son, tell me what he just said isn't true."

"It's true, I fucked up. I'm going to go talk to her when I leave here though. I need to know who them niggas is because they got to pay for what they did to her," I admitted.

"I'll ask Jayde who they were. I know she'll tell me," Joe added.

"Thanks bro." I nodded my head.

"Okay, well I'll make this quick because it sounds like you have some important shit to handle," my pops stated.

"Yeah, what's going on, Pops?" I inquired.

"So, I have a meeting set up for us when we go to Jamaica for your birthday. I'm going to introduce you to a connect there and let him know that he'll be working directly with y'all. I'm going to announce my retirement when we get back from the trip."

"Word, that's what's up Pops," I responded.

What my pops had just said was great news, but I can't bring myself to be happy about it after what happened to Bri. I got to find them niggas and make them pay now. I need to figure out a way to show her that she can count on me. I have to make this up to her. I've never felt this guilty about anything in my life.

I stayed and talked to my father and brother for a little while longer before leaving the house. I got in my car and drove straight to Bri's house. I know she said she don't want to see me, but I have to make her. I can't live with myself knowing she's possibly hurting.

I pulled up to Bri's house and parked behind her car. I got out of the car and rang Bri's doorbell. I waited for what felt like forever before someone came and opened the door.

"What are you doing here? Brielle doesn't want to see you," Stacey informed me.

"I know, but I have to see her. I need to make sure that she's fine with my own eyes."

"That's the thing, she's not fine though. She tried calling you I don't know how many times. She was in real-life pain. She damn near passed out, which is why I took her to the hospital. She's tired and stressed right now. Seeing you will only make things worse. Besides, she's sleep right now."

"Come on Stacey, I just want to see her. I won't wake her up," I promised.

Stacey sighed before stepping to the side. I walked past her and up the stairs to Bri's bedroom. She was in bed knocked out sleep. I ran my hand across her forehead and could feel that it was warm. I feel like such a fuck up right now. I know my mother gone get in my ass when she gets wind of this. She and my sister really took a liking to Bri. She hangs out with them when I'm not around and they're always calling her just to talk on the phone. It felt like I had found the one. I know I fucked up, but I can't let her leave me. I will beg and grovel for however long it takes for her to forgive me.

I sat and watched her sleep for almost two hours until Joe text and told me to meet him at the warehouse. He had my package waiting for me, better known as the guys from the club last night. He came through quicker than I expected, but I wasn't complaining. It was going to be a welcomed distraction.

"I love you Bri, and I'm sorry. I'm going to make this up to you baby," I whispered in her ear before kissing her forehead.

"You're leaving?" Stacey asked from behind me.

"Yeah, I got some business to handle. I know you might hate me right now, but I'm going to make this up to her. I never meant to hurt your sister. It was all just a misunderstanding. I don't want to stress her out more while she's sick. Can you tell her I stopped by and when she's ready to talk I'll be here?"

"Okay, can you do me a favor though?" Stacey requested.

"What's up?"

"Make whoever did this to my sister pay."

"Say less."

I left Bri's house and drove forty-five minutes to the warehouse. When I got there, Joe, Pete, and Glenn were in the back where we tortured and killed niggas. I checked the clip in my Glock before going back where they were. The four guys from the club were sitting in chairs tied up and stripped down to their boxers. They looked scared shitless. I don't know where Jayde met they asses at. They weren't shit like us.

"Do y'all know why you're here?" I calmly asked.

"No, but you can have whatever money you want," one of the guys said.

"Do it fucking look like we need your money?" I bellowed.

"No sir," one of the other guys answered.

"You're here because y'all fucking drugged the wrong woman. My woman to be exact," I advised them.

"We ain't drug no bitch," the guy snarled.

I loved when they talked shit. I reached out and hit him in his nose with the end of my gun, cracking his shit.

"Arggggh," he screamed, leaking blood.

"Now, as I was saying before I was rudely interrupted, one of you niggas drugged my woman last night while at the club. I know y'all know who I'm talking about because I beat your ass once already," I told them, looking at the one guy I fought.

"Why the fuck y'all out here drugging women? Y'all can't get pussy on y'all own?" Joe asked, disgusted.

We might be street niggas but we don't violate women in that manner. We live by the code women and children are spared, because we'd paint the system crimson if someone ever violated my mother or sister.

"I can get pussy. Your girl Jayde was about to give it up to me until y'all ass showed up last night," the nigga whose nose I broke said, causing me to shoot him in the kneecap. He didn't know when to shut the fuck up.

"Now, where was I? Oh yes, which one of you drugged my woman last night? In case you need a reminder of which one I'm talking about, I'm referring to Bri. The light-skinned woman that you were trying to force out of the club with you last night."

"Aye, wait man, I didn't drug her. I don't know what she told you, but she was begging for me to take her somewhere private. She was going with me willingly. Maybe she only told you that to try and get out of trouble," the guy that Bri was with professed.

Taking a good look at him made me realize I was tripping last night. This guy doesn't even look like Bri's type. He's a dark-skinned, slim, medium-height nigga rocking a jogging suit and a pair of Adidas. He can't even afford my woman. He's nowhere near the standards of what she would date. His appearance even rings out as he's a lame. You can't go from a nigga like me to this. I need to whoop my own ass for even thinking she wanted him. My judgment was off last night due to the liquor and pill that I popped. I got to leave that shit alone.

"Man, that bitch lying to you and you believe her. She was about to give my man some pussy then got caught, so now the hoe covering her ass and we about to pay for it," one of the other niggas ranted.

This was taking longer than I wanted. I needed to show them I wasn't playing, so without warning, I lifted my gun and shot the nigga in the center of his head, causing him to slump in his chair.

"Oh shit," his friend next to him yelped.

"Okay, now that that's out of the way. Anyone else want to disrespect my woman, or can we move on and one of you answer my question? You all know that she's not lying just like I know she isn't. So any volunteers? We can do this the easy way or the hard way."

The guys just sat there looking scared, not saying a word.

"Aight, the hard way it is." I shrugged, stepping out of the way so Glenn and Pete can handle their business. They've been a part of my team for a few years now. They're what you would call my muscle. If I needed something handled and didn't want to get my hands dirty, I used them. They had a way of getting people to talk. They pulled their tools from the drawer and got to work.

The piercing screams of the three grown men were heard throughout the room. The sound of it was deafening. Not to mention the smell of burning flesh had my stomach turning. I don't know how much more of this I can withstand. This room was going to need a good power washing when they're done.

"Okay, okay, please stop. I'll tell you whatever you want to know," the dude that was trying to leave with Bri pleaded.

"Cool, that means you other two aren't needed, so you no longer need to suffer." I nodded at Joe and he lifted his 9mm and shot both guys in the head.

"Now tell me, why would you drug Bri and there were three other girls there? Girls that I know would have given you pussy. Did she turn you down or something and you couldn't take rejection?" I questioned.

"No, it was nothing like that. I did try talking to Bri but she didn't seem interested. I was going to leave her alone, but then while she was in the bathroom, one of her friends told me that she likes to party in order to loosen up. Dave had some pills in his pocket and gave one to the girl and she put it in the drink. It wasn't even our idea to begin with," he confessed.

"Which girl was it?" I inquired.

"I don't know her name but I can give you a description of her."

"Okay, that works."

Dave gave me a full description of her and I knew exactly who he was talking about. I got mad all over again hearing that it was one of the girls behind this. That meant Bri wasn't safe in her house because someone living with her wanted to do her harm. I couldn't understand what would possess them to want to do this when she's been nothing but good to them. She's literally

the one providing a roof over their head and this is the thanks she gets.

"Thanks for speaking up," I finally said.

"No problem, does that mean I get to go now?" he asked.

"Nope," I responded before putting a bullet in his head and chest. I didn't give a fuck if it wasn't his idea or not. He and his friend went along with the shit. He knew she was drugged and he was still about to rape her, so he was in the wrong and had to pay.

Now I have to think of a way to tell Bri about the jealous bitches she's living with. There is no way this shit can slide. Jealousy is a terrible trait to have. It makes you do the unthinkable, not realizing the consequences, and sometimes the consequences just might be death.

CHAPTER ONE

BRIELLE

Two weeks have passed since I last spoke to Khalil. He was calling me all day every day and showing up at my house to the point where I had to block his ass. Stacey had to threaten to call the police for him to stop showing up at the house. I've been going on with my life as usual, but I'd be lying if I said I didn't miss him.

I kind of want to sit down and talk to him about what happened, but on the other hand, I want to say fuck him. I understand how things looked but he should have known that something wasn't right. I would never pull the shit that he did. Then to make matters worse, I'm pregnant and still don't know how I feel about that.

This is one of those when it rains it pours situations in my life. I went from everything being good and to everything going bad all at once. I still need to figure out what to do about my roommate situation. At this point, I want to kick everybody out, but at the same time the money was coming in handy from them. If I kick everybody out then I'm going to be stuck paying for everything on my own. I would have to actually get a full-time job and that's not in my cards right now.

I can't go to school full time, work full time, and take care of a baby. That's if I even keep this baby. I never planned on being a single mother. At least when I was pregnant by Troy I knew that he was going to help me and I wouldn't have to do everything on my own. He wanted a baby just as much as I did. I don't know if Khalil wants a child. I would think he would have had one already if he wanted them since he had been with Krystal so long and he's about to be twenty-six.

There's so many decisions that I need to make in such a short time. I wish I could just hide under a rock but I need to put my big girl pants on. Not to mention our trip to Jamaica is in two weeks and everything is paid for. My family is looking forward to the trip and so was I. It's going to be my twenty-first birthday and I was ready to enjoy it to the fullest. Things would be awkward going on the trip without us making up first. Well, not so much as making up but getting on speaking terms. It's going to take some time for me to forgive Khalil and work on a relationship with him. We've only been together for six months and I'm already dealing with cheating. If it wasn't a baby involved I'd probably just allow him to take me on the trip. I'd get some birthday dick then go about my life. Unfortunately, things aren't that simple.

I brushed my hair into a ponytail, grabbed my purse and phone, then headed down the stairs. The living room was quiet since everybody was out except for Stacey. What was supposed to be a couple days turned into a couple weeks of her being here. Ever since everything went down she hasn't left my side. She doesn't trust me being alone with the girls. She still believes the girls have something to do with what happened and I don't know what I believe. I'd hate to think the people I'm supposed to trust would do anything to harm me. I've slept under the same roof as them for almost a year. Things have been awkward as hell, especially between me and Ryan. I don't want to get in the middle of what's going on between her and Stacey. I love them both like a sister and Stacey is actually my blood.

"Are you sure that you don't want me to go with you?" Stacey asked for the third time today.

"I love you Stace, but I'll be fine. I'm going to only be gone for a couple hours. You don't have to worry about me."

"I love you too, and I can't help it. It's a lot going on with you. Khalil might pop up at the school, then what?"

"He's not going to show up there. It's not like he has a copy of my tutoring schedule."

"Okay, if you need anything call and let me know."

"I will, just relax and I'll see you soon," I told her before walking out of the house.

I was glad that me and my sister were able to rebuild our relationship, but at the same time I feel like she's smothering me. I know that she means well so I'm not tripping. If something happened to her like it did to me, I'd probably be the same way.

I climbed in my car and immediately turned the air on. It was 80 degrees out here but the humidity felt like a hundred. This was the only the only thing I hated about living in the south. I've lived out here all my life but I've never gotten used to the heat. During the summer months I spend as much time in the house as possible until the sun goes down. Today is actually the first day that I'm leaving the house after everything that happened. I've been trying to avoid running into anybody.

I need gas but at the same time I don't want to be late for my session, so I headed to the school first. I parked in the lot then grabbed my book bag and headed inside to the library. I looked around until I found Darrius sitting at the table scrolling through his phone. When he felt my presence he looked up and smiled, showing all his teeth. He was a light-skin handsome man but he didn't have shit on Khalil. He was also more on the slim side and I wasn't really into that. I got used to Khalil's muscular build.

"Hey Bri, how are you?"

"I'm fine and you?"

"Oh, you're definitely fine, but I asked how you were doing not how you looked." He smirked.

I couldn't help but laugh at how corny that statement was as I sat down across from him. I've been tutoring him for a couple months now and every time he had a corny statement or joke that makes me laugh. That's about as far as it goes though, because he has a girlfriend and I was with Khalil. He's super cool though and a good person to talk to. Usually he'd come by the house to study or we'd end up at Starbucks, but since it's a little later than when we normally get together we chose the school.

"Are you ready to get started?" I asked, pulling out the trigonometry book.

"I'm always ready," he replied, looking up at me with a smile. He was being extra flirtatious today but I brushed it off because it all seemed innocent.

We sat and studied for two hours then I was ready to call it a night. We went over his trig and social science. He should be well prepared for his quiz. I was going to take summer courses at first but then I changed my mind. With everything that's been going on I'm glad that I didn't pick up classes because there's no way I'd be able to focus.

Darrius picked up my bag then walked me out to my car. He waited until I pulled off before walking over to his.

I was halfway home when my gas light came on,

reminding me that I need gas. I sighed as I drove another block and pulled into the nearest BP. Khalil would get in my ass if he knew I was at the gas station by myself at night. I haven't pumped gas since I met Khalil. He either took my car to get gas or he'd meet me at the gas station and come pump it for me. He made sure to remind me all the time that all kinds of shit can happen at a gas station at night and it wasn't meant for a female to be there on their own. I shrugged those thoughts off and got out of my car. It wasn't like I was going to call Khalil to come pump my gas for me and my car doesn't run on air.

I climbed out of the car and looked around, checking out my surroundings before going inside the gas station. Morning sickness has been kicking my ass so I grabbed a couple Gatorades, ginger ale ,and chicken flavor Ramen noodles. I hate noodles but that and jello are the only two things that don't make me vomit. My doctor gave me some pills that's supposed to help with the morning sickness but they don't work at all. I'm still waking up in the morning throwing up and queasy throughout the day. I don't know how long this is supposed to last but I need it to stop.

I got in line and waited patiently for the people in front of me to pay for their things. I was next in line when the man in front of me started being difficult.

"Dude, I gave you a 20 so give me my fucking change," he cussed at the clerk.

"You gave me a 10 not a 20," the clerk yelled.

"No, I gave you a 20. You better check that damn camera," the guy bellowed, slamming his fist on the counter.

"Get out or me call the police," the clerk threatened in broken English.

"Man, this why I hate coming to this damn store. It's always some broke nigga on some bullshit," the guy behind me grumbled, getting the man's attention causing him to turn around.

"Who the fuck you calling broke? I'll take all the money you got in your pockets right now."

"Man, be easy, I'm just trying to get out of here. My shorty at home waiting on me and I don't want her to think I'm out on some bullshit," the guy behind me explained.

"Fuck you and your insecure bitch. I want my damn money and I'm not going anywhere until I get it," he ranted.

I don't know how much change dude was supposed to get back but at this point, I was ready to give his ass a 20 out my purse so that I could pay for my shit and go. My bladder was feeling like it was going to explode. I don't know why I didn't use the bathroom before leaving the library after drinking two bottles of water.

"Now, back to you, stupid bitch. Open the register and give me my money," he demanded, turning his attention back to the clerk.

"Get out, me call police now," the clerk warned, picking up the phone. Before he could press the number 9, dude pulled a gun from his waist and pointed it at the man.

"Oh shit," I yelled, running toward the door.

"Don't fucking move or I'll shoot," he threatened us.

I stopped in my tracks and watched as dude kicked in the door that led to the back where the clerk was. He knocked the register off the counter, causing it to break open. He wasted no time grabbing all the bills and rushing out of the gas station.

I didn't want to be a witness to shit so I rushed out behind the guy before the clerk had a chance to call the police. This was the wildest shit I had ever experienced. All because he didn't get his change. I'm starting to think he only gave the clerk a 10 and he needed an excuse to rob the place.

I hurriedly got in my car and pulled off. I still needed gas so

I drove up the street to the Special K. This time I was just going to pay at the pump and not go in. After all, I did just get all my stuff for free.

While I was waiting for my tank to fill I noticed a van pull into the pump behind me. I was starting to get nervous after what just happened at the other gas station, so I pulled out my phone to call my sister.

"Hey, where are you? I was just about to call and check on you," Stacey said.

"Hey girl, I needed gas and it was some bullshit, so I had to go to another station. A van just pulled in here and I got nervous. It's probably nothing," I replied.

"Well, stay on the phone with me until you get here. It's better to be safe than sorry," she reminded me.

I stayed on the phone listening to Stacey talk. Once my pump clicked I put it back and tightened the cap. Just as I was about to get in my car, somebody rushed toward me and grabbed me by my ponytail, causing my phone to fall.

"Stacey! Call 911—" I yelled before my mouth was covered. I was struggling to get free but I wasn't going down without a fight. He pulled me again as the driver of the van drove on the side of us. He threw me in the van and climbed in, closing the door behind him. The guy in the passenger seat jumped out and I could see him running toward my car and climbing in. I was confused as hell about what was going on. If this was a carjacking then why the hell did they throw me in this van?

Tears instantly fell from my eyes. All I could think was that I should have listened to Khalil then none of this would be happening. My sadness quickly turned to anger because I blamed him. If he hadn't fucked up I wouldn't be getting gas on my own and my gas would have never got this low.

"Stop crying, beautiful," a guy said, using his finger to wipe away my tears.

My head immediately shot up when I noticed it was the guy from the BP. I swallowed the lump in my throat because he was about to kill me for being a witness to him robbing the store.

"Look, you don't have to kill me. I won't tell anyone about what happened tonight," I promised.

"I'm not worried about you saying anything and I'm not going to kill you."

"Then what do you want with me?"

"It's a secret." He smirked.

The first thing that came to mind was these niggas were about to gang rape me and there wasn't shit that I could do about it.

We drove for I don't know how long before the van came to a stop. They had blindfolded me about ten minutes ago, so I couldn't see where we were at.

I could hear shuffling before I was pulled out of the van by my arm.

I wasn't about to make it easy for these niggas to hurt me so flight or fight kicked in. Using my free arm, I swung, punching him in the nose causing him to release his grip from my arm. I used that as my opportunity to get away and remove my blindfold.

I started running and ran straight into some cock diesel nigga. His chest was hard as a rock. I damn near hit the ground but he grabbed me, stopping me from falling. Under any other circumstances I would appreciate being wrapped in a pair of strong arms, but not this time. If he was here he was probably in line to rape me too. Thinking about that caused me to wiggle in his arms, but he wasn't budging. I guess I was irritating him so he picked me up as if I was light as a feather and carried me inside the building. I was carried down a long hall where a man was standing outside a door. The man opened the door, allowing the guy to walk in with me.

Just when I thought my life couldn't get any worse, I'm kidnapped. These niggas was about to get the chance to have their way with me and there's nothing I could do about it. All I could think about was my unborn child and whether it would make it through this. Here I was earlier having doubts about going through this pregnancy, and now all I can think about is protecting it with my life.

The guy placed me down on my feet and walked out of the room. I could hear the lock click from the outside. Looking around the room, it was a lot cleaner than I expected. It had a queen-size bed, dresser, chair, mini fridge, and a TV mounted on the wall. There was another door in the room, so of course my nosey ass twisted the knob. It was a full bathroom behind the door. I was glad about that because I still needed to pee. I released my bladder then flushed the toilet and washed my hands.

Once I finished in the bathroom I sat on the bed and turned on the TV. I hope Stacey called the police in time. Maybe they could track my car to wherever it was taken to. All I can do now is sit down and see what happens next. It's not like I can break out of this room and take down all these men with my fists.

CHAPTER TWO

KHALIL

As I sat outside my warehouse my mind was going a mile a minute. I was nervous as hell about getting out of my car and going inside. I was wondering if I had just made things go from bad to worse between me and Bri. The way I looked at it, she left me with no choice. I tried calling and showing up to her house so that we could talk calmly but she wasn't cooperating with me. She had my back up against the wall. I couldn't just let her leave me without us at least talking first.

A knock on my window pulled me away from my thoughts. Looking up, I saw that it was Joe. Reluctantly, I let the window down. I already knew how this conversation was about to go.

"Nigga, why you just sitting out here in the car? Go in there and talk to that girl. I know she's scared as hell right now. I told your dumb ass not to go through with this."

"Shut the fuck up. I did what I thought was best given the circumstances."

"Man, you sound dumb as hell right now. Who the fuck

kidnaps their girl because she's not talking to them? You could have waited until she was ready to talk."

"When the hell was that going to be? I gave her ass two fucking weeks. I got tired of waiting."

"You have to think about how she feels. You was cheating on her while she was drugged, then she was in the hospital and you ignored all her calls."

"Look Dr. Phil, don't stand here and act like you ain't out here cheating on Kenya. You was just with Jayde a few days ago."

"That's beside the point. I ain't never kidnapped Kenya or no other bitch for not talking to me. Sitting in this car not going to solve shit. Your only two options is to let somebody drop Bri off somewhere and act like this never happened or go in there and let your girl know that you're a psycho."

I thought about what Joe said and I was going to go with option two. I couldn't risk somebody dropping Bri off and me not seeing her still. If I did that then all of this would have been for nothing.

I let my window back up and got out of the car. Walking into the warehouse, I spoke to a few of the guys then walked to the back where they were keeping Bri at. It was actually my personal room that I sleep in when I work late and don't feel like driving home.

When I made it to the door I sent the guys away. I didn't want them to hear me and Bri arguing. I don't be telling these niggas my business. Joe is the only one that knows everything that went down.

Pulling my key from my pocket, I put it in and unlocked the door. Pushing the door open, Bri was sprawled out in the bed sleep. I grabbed the chair and sat down in front of her. I didn't want to wake her and piss her off even more. I know how much she hates being woke out of her sleep.

I was actually tired as hell myself. I've been in Memphis for the last four days taking caring of business. My plan was to come home and get some rest, but as I was boarding the plane Adam hit me up and told me that they saw Bri alone. I had them looking out for her since she didn't want to see me. It was never my intentions to kidnap her when I had them looking out for her. I just wanted to make sure she was good.

Every time they checked in they told me that she didn't leave the house, so when they told me she was out today and at the gas station alone at night my mind went somewhere else. She was putting her life in danger and I didn't like that. I just wanted to be able to get through to her the real dangers of that.

I sat watching Bri, not realizing I nodded off until I felt my chair being kicked. Opening my eyes, I was face to face with an angry Bri. The look in her eyes was one that I'd never experienced from a woman. From the look of things, I should have went with option one that Joe suggested. Bri looked like she was ready to tear into my ass.

"What the fuck are you doing sitting here sleep, Khalil? How did you even get here? Where the fuck is here?" she rattled off question after question.

"Before you get mad, I did this for us," I assured her.

"Before I get mad? Nigga, I'm past mad, I know you didn't have some of your workers to kidnap me?"

Running my hands across my face, I sighed before opening my mouth to explain everything to Bri.

"This is my warehouse and the guys that kidnapped you work for me. You was never in any real danger. I just wanted to get you alone so that we could talk," I explained.

Bri looked at me, frozen in place for a moment. Like she was allowing what I said to register. Before I could react, she started punching me. Her ass was hitting me hard as hell as tears fell from her eyes. I allowed her to get a few more licks in before pulling her into a bear hug. She allowed me to hold her for a couple minutes before snatching away.

I thought she was done and ready to talk until she reached out and slapped the shit out of me. It took everything in me not to snatch her ass up. I deserved it though, so I let it slide this time, but this will be the last time she gets a chance to put her hands on me. I don't play that hitting shit because if I hit her ass back then I'd be wrong.

Bri paced the floor back and forth trying to gather her thoughts. I remained quiet to give her a chance to calm down. I didn't want to say the wrong thing to make her go off on a rant again.

"Are you out of your fucking mind, Khalil? How could you let your guys kidnap me? Do you know how I felt? There was all kind of thoughts going through my mind. I thought those niggas was going to rape and kill me because I witnessed one of them robbing a gas station. He had a gun pointed at me and you're talking about I was in no danger," she stated.

Hearing that last part caused me to jump from my seat. I ain't know shit about nobody robbing a gas station let alone pulling a gun out on her.

"Who robbed the gas station and pulled a gun out on you?" I asked.

"Nigga, I don't know, I didn't ask his name. He was tall, dark skinned, chubby with a short haircut."

I already knew who she was describing. She was talking about Max. He was one of the stickup boys and hittas on my team. He's always been loyal but I can't let him off the hook with pulling a gun out on Bri. I told them to do what was needed to get her but not to bring her any harm. He wasn't supposed to scare her like that.

"I'm sorry that he did that. I promise I didn't tell him to

pull a gun out on you. I'll handle him once we're finished talking."

"What do you want to talk about? You cheated and then kidnapped me. Am I just supposed to forgive you for that?"

"I'm not asking you to forgive me right now. I just want to talk to you. I tried doing it the right way but that wasn't working for you."

"Go ahead, say what's on your mind," Bri sighed, sitting on the edge of the bed.

"Okay, first I want to say sorry about everything. I know I fucked up by sleeping with Krystal but it didn't mean shit. That was the first time I touched her since we got together. I was just mad and acted stupid. I allowed my pride to get in the way that night. I was drunk and pissed that you allowed a nigga to touch you when I had only been about you that entire time."

"Nigga, I was fucking drugged. You should have trusted me and known that something was off. You knew everything that I been through and you was the first man I gave a chance since Troy died, so why would I just willingly try to fuck another nigga?"

"I don't know Bri, I wasn't thinking. As soon as it was done, I felt bad as hell and went home," I partially lied. She didn't need to know that I spent the night and had a round two. She definitely didn't need to know that I fucked Krystal raw.

"Do you think that makes me feel better that you felt bad? I felt bad as hell finding out that I was drugged. I tried calling you while I was in the hospital and you weren't there. You was supposed to be the one person that I could count on. I thought that we were better than that, but I guess I was wrong," she stated solemnly as tears fell from her eyes.

I felt like shit and wanted to wrap her in my arms but that might only cause her to swing on me again.

"I know Bri, and if you give me a chance I'll do whatever it takes to make this all up to you. You're the only woman that I want to be with. I love you and I want to continue to show you the world. At least let me take you to Jamaica still."

"I don't know Khalil. I need to think about this. All I needed was some time then I was going to talk to you about us, but then you went and kidnapped now you got me wondering if you got some screws loose."

"I know, I wasn't thinking. I just panicked, but I really needed to talk to you about something else that's more important than us being together."

Bri looked at me skeptically before opening her mouth to speak.

"Okay, what's so important?"

"Joe was the one that told me what happened to you. After I found out I had some of my guys find the niggas that y'all was at the club with. One of them told me that Lena put the drugs in your drink but Jayde and Ryan sat there and watched her do it."

"Damn, Stacey was right. She said one of the girls had drugged me but out of all of them I would have expected Jayde. Are you sure it was Lena and Ryan that saw them do it?" she asked to be sure.

"Yes, he described Lena to me and said that all of them was there."

"Are you sure? Why would he just voluntarily give you that information?" she asked skeptically.

"Don't worry about how I got the information, just know that what I'm telling you is true. Them hoes can't be trusted and you need to get them up out your house," I advised her.

"Thanks for letting me know, now can I get my car so that I can go home?"

"So we're not going to talk about us?"

"No, not right now. I just need to handle the issues with my roommates and clear my head. You can come over tomorrow, well later on today, after 4 so that we can talk."

"Okay cool, I'll let you know when I'm on my way," I replied. I didn't want to wait but I'll take what I can get.

I got up from the chair and walked Bri out of the room. We walked down the hall and some of the guys was sitting around talking. I grabbed Bri's key fob from the table then walked her outside to her car.

I waited for her to pull off before going back in the warehouse. I walked around until I found Max talking to Joe. Without hesitation, I reached out and slammed my fist into his jaw, causing him to stumble and Joe to jump back.

"Man, what the hell was that for?" Max asked, holding his jaw.

"That's for pulling a gun out on my girl. You lucky I don't put a bullet in your ass. The next time you see me with her, you gone apologize for that shit," I told him.

"Nigga, you did what?" Joe inquired.

"This dumb ass nigga robbed a gas station and pulled a gun out on Bri," I answered.

"Boss man, I didn't plan on doing that. It just happened. The cashier was on some bullshit and I didn't want her to run and get away from us, so I just pulled it out to stall her," he explained.

"I don't give a fuck. Don't let that shit happen again," I warned him before walking away. I had no plans on doing any work, so I left the warehouse and headed home to get some sleep.

CHAPTER THREE
BRIELLE

The drive to my house felt like it was long as hell when it was only about thirty minutes. I still can't believe Khalil's crazy ass kidnapped me. I knew he was kind of on the crazy side but not crazy like this. I mean, who the fuck kidnaps someone that they're supposed to love and want to be with? I wanted to sit down and work on things with him at first but now I'm skeptical as hell.

When I pulled up to my house all the lights were on, which was odd since it was almost four in the morning. I grabbed my purse and got out of the car locking my door behind me. I took my key from my purse and was about to put it into the lock when the front door was swung open.

"What the hell Brielle? Where have you been? You had me worried about you. I called the police and everything," Stacey rambled.

"I'm sorry, it's a long story," I replied, walking in the house.

"No bitch, I'm not letting you off that easy," my sister told me.

"Okay, it's been a long night. Just come up to my room then," I said, walking up the stairs to my bedroom.

I took my shoes off then started stripping out of my clothes, not caring that Stacey was standing there. I threw on one of my pajama sets then climbed in bed. Stacey climbed in right next to me not taking her eyes off me. There was a look of anger and relief all in one. I can only imagine how she must have felt all that time while I was gone.

"You're in your bed comfortable now, so tell me what the hell is going on because you look perfectly fine to me," Stacey asked with her impatient ass.

"Okay, so after I left the tutoring session I stopped to get gas. Somebody in the store was acting an ass and ended up robbing it. I ran out after that without getting gas so I went to another gas station. That's when I called you because I saw a van. When I was getting in the car somebody came up behind me and that's when I told you to call the police. My phone fell and somebody snatched me into the van and drove me somewhere. I just knew these niggas was about to beat and rape me when they locked me in a bedroom."

"Oh my god Brielle, that is so crazy, I'm sorry that happened to you. How did you get away?" Stacey inquired, cutting me off as tears fell from her already red eyes.

I felt bad that my sister was worried and crying all this time when I was fine.

"Girl, I was about to get to that part. I ended up falling asleep for a couple hours and when I woke up Khalil was in the room staring at me."

"Awwww, your man came to rescue you. You have to forgive him now," Stacey beamed.

"No bitch, that nigga had me kidnapped so that we could talk. Those were his guys that kidnapped me and that was his warehouse that they took me to," I explained.

Stacey's facial expression changed in the blink of an eye. She went from being excited that he saved me to being angry.

"Oh hell no, I'm going to beat his ass when I see him. Why would he do some shit like that?"

"His dumb ass said that I gave him no choice since I wasn't answering his calls. He missed me and really needed to see me."

"Okay now, that's kind of hot. Did you give him some?"

"Girl no, I beat his ass. I was scared as hell before I found out what was going on. I'm convinced that he's a psycho."

"Nah, he loves your mean ass. Ain't no man ever took those measures to get my attention before. That's going to be your husband one day."

"Girl, I ain't thinking about that right now. I did tell him he can come over later today so that we can talk."

"Okay, I know that you're going to take him back but make him sweat first," Stacey advised me.

"I'm going to give him another chance. He just doesn't know that yet. I'm going to make him pay up first."

"Shit, I know that's right. He can afford it. If I was you I'd make his ass take you shopping to buy new clothes for Jamaica."

I laughed at Stacey's response because that was already part of the plan. When Khalil and I first agreed on Jamaica he said shopping was included.

Stacey and I talked for a few more minutes about the trip to Jamaica before I finally decided to open up about what Khalil told me. I was nervous about telling her because I already know she's going to flip out.

"Look, I'm about to tell you something but you're going to have to stay calm," I said.

"Nah, it depends on what it is because from the look on your face, it doesn't seem good."

I sighed before responding because there was no way she was about to be calm.

"So you were right about the girls having something to do with what happened to me. Lena got the drugs from one of the guys and put it in my drink while Jayde and Ryan sat back doing nothing."

"I knew it, them bitches ain't shit," Stacey yelled, jumping up from the bed.

"Stacey don't, it's been a long night. I just want to go to bed," I protested.

"So your ass just going to let this shit slide?"

"No, I want to get some sleep then talk about it when I get up."

"Okay, but they're definitely not getting off the hook." Stacey stayed reluctantly.

Stacey calmed down then climbed in bed with me. I'm guessing she planned on sleeping in here tonight and not in my office where she's been sleeping the last couple of weeks. I bought a futon and put it in there so that she could have her own space because the couch in my living room was not made for people to sleep on.

I woke up around noon and Stacey was still sleep, so I grabbed my phone and slid out bed. Going into the bathroom, I closed the door and sat down on the toilet. I saw a text from Khalil asking if I ate yet. I replied back letting him know I hadn't and that I just woke up.

Putting my phone down, I finished taking care of my business then climbed in the shower. I took a much needed twenty-minute shower then brushed my teeth and washed my face. I wrapped a towel around me then went into my bedroom. I moisturized my body then got dressed in a short red sundress. I didn't have plans on going anywhere but Khalil was coming over so I wanted to look semi cute.

I brushed my hair into a bun then applied a light coat of lip gloss and eyeliner. Just as I was about to sit down my stomach began to growl, reminding me that I hadn't eaten since yesterday evening. I really have to do better because I know I'm starving my poor baby.

Instead of sitting down, I grabbed my car key and headed down the stairs so that I could get the stuff I got from the gas station last night.

As I was opening the front door Khalil was walking up with bags of food from American Del. I know I told him to come after three.

"Hey, you said you hadn't eaten yet so I figured you might be hungry. I can leave and come back later though like we planned."

He was here already and thoughtful enough to bring me food so I stepped to the side and allowed Khalil to walk in.

I led the way to the dining room and got some plates for us and my sister. Pulling the containers of food out of the bags, I opened them and looked inside. There were wings, tenders, fries, and a Philly cheesesteak.

"Thanks for the food but why did you buy so much?" I asked, looking down at everything.

"I didn't know what you wanted and I figured that you was going to share with your sister so I wanted to make sure you had enough," he explained.

"Well, wasn't that thoughtful of you. Me and Stacey not going to eat all of this so you might as well put some on a plate too.

Looking at the food, I grabbed a few fries, a honey hot tender, and cut a piece of the Philly steak. My stomach is bigger than my eyes right now. I'm hungry but I know I can't overdo it.

Khalil and I sat and made small talk while we were eating.

He was pretty much catching me up on what had been going on with him. We weren't going to talk about anything deep until we went to my room and talked in private.

I was halfway done eating when Jayde and Lena came walking into the dining room.

"Why you ain't tell nobody you was ordering food?" Jayde asked with an attitude.

"Clearly you see Khalil sitting here so maybe, just maybe, he brought food with him. It's not up to me to tell him to bring food for everybody," I responded sarcastically.

I wasn't in the mood to deal with Jayde's shit right now. I was trying to wait for everyone to come down so that I could talk about what happened. I wanted to take care of all of this before Khalil came over.

Jayde was about to respond when the sound of the doorbell went off. I was about to get up and answer it, but Stacey came down the stairs at the same time so she opened it then stepped to the side to let Joe in.

He spoke to her then headed this way with Stacey. She opened her mouth like she was about to say something, but it was like something clicked in her mind. Before any of us could react, she reached out and punched Lena in the face. Lena tried to swing back but Stacey was too fast for her. She was sending blow after blow, calling Lena all kinds of stupid bitches.

"Bitch, get the fuck off my cousin," Jayde yelled, jumping in.

Pregnant or not, I couldn't let my sister get jumped even though she was winning, so I started throwing blows Jayde's way. We was in a full-on fight until Ryan came down. Instead of trying to pull Jayde off Stacey she pulled me, causing me to turn around and swing on her ass because that was some suspect shit.

Ryan grabbed me by hair, almost pulling me down until

Khalil stepped in pulling her off of me. They gave me time to pull Jayde off of my sister and Joe pulled Stacey off of Lena.

"What the fuck, Brielle? You showing out in front of your nigga and sister now? Since when do we fight like this?" Ryan asked, sounding hurt.

"Miss me with that shit Ryan. Since when do we sit back and allow bitches to put us in harm?" I countered.

"What are you talking about?" Ryan questioned, confused.

"I'm talking about the fact that you sat there and allowed Lena to put drugs in my drink then you acted like nothing happened the next day. I expected that from them bitches but not you. I thought we were better than that," I cried. I was so angry I could feel a headache coming on already.

"Brielle, I'm so sorry, it wasn't like that. You was never supposed to get hurt. It was just to help loosen you up a little. We were going to look out for you," Ryan advised me.

I looked at her like she was stupid. This was the second time I heard that dumb ass shit. I'm confused and surrounded around idiots. People putting my life in danger but then acting like I would be fine.

"What do you mean you was going to watch me? I almost left and fucked another nigga without even realizing what was going on. Had Khalil not showed up, no telling what would have happened. Not to mention I ended up in the hospital because of that shit. Talking about I need to loosen up, like I'm not the same person I was when we first met," I pointed out.

"I know, I swear it went further than we expected. None of us wanted to hurt you. Well, at least I didn't," Ryan replied.

I massaged my temples to try and calm down. All kinds of crazy thoughts were going through my head because I don't know how we were going to come back from any of this. I was too irritated to think about anything so I headed upstairs to my bedroom.

I know I told Khalil that we can discuss us but I don't have the energy. Then on top of that, all three of them paid their way to Jamaica so the trip was about to be awkward as hell. There's nothing I can do about that though because it's nonre-fundable.

The last thing I need to do while pregnant is stress so I'm not making any decisions about anything until after I come back. Hopefully the trip will help relax and ease my mind so that I can think things through clearly. As I was climbing in the bed there was a knock at the door.

"Come in," I grumbled as I looked around for my remote.

"Are you okay?" Khalil asked, walking in closing the door behind him.

"No, I'm not, everything is so fucked up right now. I haven't been this stressed since my ex died," I admitted.

"I'm sorry that you're going through this and that I'm partially to blame," he apologized.

"Thanks, I know that I said we could discuss us but right now isn't the time. I have a lot of thinking to do. I'm still going to Jamaica though and you're still buying my clothes. We're going to enjoy ourselves then we'll discuss everything when I get back," I told him.

"Okay, whatever you want, you got it. I'll send you my credit card details," he replied without hesitating, causing me to smile.

Khalil locked the bedroom door then walked over to where I was, licking his lips.

"Don't even think about it. I'm not about to fuck you. You need to go get tested before you put your dick anywhere near me," I advised him.

"Okay, let me just lay with you for a minute. We don't have to have sex," he said, climbing in bed next to me.

Leaning over, he placed a kiss on my neck, repeatedly

saying how sorry he is. The shit was feeling good as hell. He was sucking, biting, and licking all over my neck. My pussy was thumping and I wanted more, but I wasn't about to let him off the hook and fuck me. First of all, I wasn't ready to go there with him yet because that was letting him off the hook too easily. Secondly, I was serious about not giving him none until after he get tested. Ain't no telling who else Krystal had been fucking before he slid up inside of her.

He took his shirt off then sat up in the bed. He lifted my dress slowly then pulled my underwear down. He sat staring at my bare pussy without saying anything,

"Are you just going to stare or are you going to taste it?" I asked impatiently. I wasn't ready to have sex with him but that didn't mean he couldn't give me no head. My hormones are all over the place and I need to cum. My vibrator don't have shit on Khalil's tongue.

Without responding, he opened my legs and got into the sniper position. His warm lips grazed my pussy, causing a moan to escape my lips. He moved his tongue inside of me then slid his tongue down to my clit. I tried not to moan loud but the shit was feeling good as hell. He hadn't even been down there for two minutes and I was close to cumming. I started backing away but he wasn't letting up. He stuck one of his thick fingers inside of me as he sucked my soul out of my body.

"Khalil wait, I'm about to cum," I cried out as my body began to shake. It wouldn't surprise me if the whole house heard me. Usually I'd mind but today I didn't care. I just wanted to bust all over his face.

He slapped me on my pussy, causing me to squirt. I held my head back and waited while he licked me clean.

"You feeling better now?"

"Yes, thank you! I needed that," I mumbled.

"You sure? 'Cause I can let you bust another one."

"Nah, I'm good, now you got me ready to pass out," I admitted.

Khalil climbed out of bed and went inside my bathroom. A couple minutes later he came back with a towel. I reached out to get it but he slapped my hand away. He wiped me clean then went back into the bathroom. I watched as he brushed his teeth. I wanted to feel him inside of me so bad but I just couldn't do it.

Once he finished brushing his teeth he came and laid down, pulling me in his arms. No lie, I missed how his strong arms felt around me.

"I'm so sorry I fucked up things between us. I promise I'm going to make things back right with us and I'm going to gain your trust back."

"You don't have to keep apologizing. I understand that you're sorry but you're definitely going to have to work hard to gain my trust back."

"I know and I will. I love you Brielle."

"I love you too Khalil," I replied back honestly. Even though I wasn't fucking with him like that right now, that doesn't change the fact that he's a good man and I love him. I thought about telling him that I was pregnant right now but the words just wouldn't leave my mouth. Part of me was scared that he wouldn't want the baby and the mood we had just set would be ruined.

CHAPTER FOUR
STACEY

Brielle stormed upstairs, leaving me down here with everybody. I wasn't worried about them trying anything. I was pissed as hell that she jumped into the fight knowing that she was pregnant. Even with the help of Jayde, Lena still got her ass whooped and I was getting licks in on Jayde too.

Ryan's explanation sounded stupid as hell. Who the fuck drugs their friend to have fun? These are by far the dumbest bitches I've ever met. Accident or not, Lena deserved that ass whooping and I wasn't allowing what she did to my sister slide.

Originally I was going to allow Bri to have her lil' meeting like she planned, but looking at Lena pissed me off. It brought back all the memories of me sitting in the hospital with Bri and I just snapped. Honestly, I don't give a fuck if she let them stay here afterward or not, because Lena got the ass whooping that she deserved. I bet none of they asses pull no shit like that again, especially with Bri.

Brielle and I might not have always seen eye to eye but

that's my blood. The only sister I got so I'm riding with her regardless. I'm the only bitch that can get away with fighting her. All these other hoes gone learn to respect her if I have to beat it out of their ass.

I went in the bathroom to check myself out to make sure that I looked straight. There wasn't a scratch or strand of hair of place. I smiled at that because Lena and Jayde were weak. How the hell you try to jump in and don't even leave a scratch? My first mind was to go out there and whoop Jayde's ass, but I'm sure the few punches I swung her way taught her a lesson. She should have learned from the last time I fought her that I wasn't one to be played with. At the same time, I can't be mad at her for sticking up for her cousin because if my sister was getting her ass beat, I'm jumping in whether it was one on one or not, and I dare a bitch to say something about it.

I left the bathroom and headed upstairs to Bri's room. I was about to knock when I heard her moaning, so I turned around and went back down the stairs. She did all that talk this morning about making him pay and not letting him off the hook that easily to only be in there moaning his name right now. I ain't even mad at her though. At least one of us getting some. I ain't had no dick in almost a month now.

Walking in the living room, I sat on the couch and turned the TV on. As I was flipping through the channels Joe came and sat down next to me. When I say next to me, I mean right up under me like this wasn't a big ass sectional. I could smell the Spearmint gum on his breath and his Dior Sauvage cologne was smelling good as hell.

"Uhm, can I help you?" I asked, looking at him.

"You can help me in more way than one, baby." He smirked.

"Joe, I promise you don't want these problems. You wouldn't know what to do with me," I replied.

"You'd be surprised what I can do. You better be lucky you Brielle's sister."

"No, you better be lucky I'm Brielle's sister. I'll have you stalking Bri trying to get to me. I can guarantee you that you ain't been with a bitch like me. You see my sister got your brother kidnapping her just for his attention. I'll have y'all fitted for matching straight jackets," I warned him.

"Oh, you got jokes I see. I take that as a challenge ma," he chuckled.

"Take it however way you want. Just know that I warned you." I shrugged before going back to watch TV. There was no need to continue the conversation we were having. The sexual tension was thick and we both knew what time it was. The ball was in his court to make a move when he was ready.

I turned around and saw that Jayde was staring a hole into the back of my head. She better be lucky I didn't feel like being petty or I'd take him into that office right now and put it down on his ass, making sure she heard everything. I think getting her ass beat in front of him was embarrassing enough for the day.

"Can you turn on the game?"

"Yeah, here's the remote," I told him, getting up from the couch.

"Where you going? I like your company," he replied, pulling me back down.

"I'm going to warm my food up and then I'm going to my room to give you and your girl some privacy."

"That's not my girl and I haven't fucked with her since everything went down with your sister. I ain't like that shit and I don't fuck with shady bitches. I came over here to make sure Bri was good and to see you," he confessed, causing me to slightly smile.

"If you were so worried about Brielle, why did you let your brother kidnap her?" I inquired.

"I didn't know he was going to do that dumb shit until it was too late or I would have warned her. By the time I found out what was happening, them dumb ass niggas was on the way to the warehouse with her and we were on the plane at the time."

I looked at him for a minute and could tell he was telling the truth. That was good because that meant he wasn't as crazy as his brother. I like crazy but only to a certain extent.

We sat and watched the game while talking about random things. Joe was actually a cool ass guy. He could be a good friend with benefits but I don't know about someone I would get in a relationship. He was fucking with Jayde after all, so that says a lot about his type and character.

A couple hours passed when Bri and Khalil came walking down the stairs. She was going to have to give me details on what made her forgive him so quick. I'm not judging her at all I'm just curious.

"Did y'all eat all the food Stace?" Bri asked.

"Nah, I put the containers in the microwave," I replied.

"So you gone just keep ignoring me Bri? You ain't take none of my calls today and you're acting like I'm not here," Joe cut in.

"Yeah, because I don't like sneaky shit. Even though me and your brother weren't on good terms, you stayed in touch checking on me. I thought we were cool but then you let some of your guys kidnap me."

"Come on now Bri, you can't be mad at me for that. I didn't know that he had that planned. If I knew ahead of time I would have tried to stop him or warn you. Brother or not, I told him what he was doing wasn't cool," Joe admitted.

"He's telling the truth. Don't be mad at him. He tried to warn me but it was too late," Khalil added.

"Okay, I'll let you off the hook and give you another chance since I'm willing to forgive Khalil for doing it," Bri replied skeptically.

We all sat around talking for a few minutes before Jayde and Lena came down the stairs together. They were acting like they were scared to come down here alone. They don't have to worry about me doing nothing to them. I already proved my point.

"Jayde, stop staring at me. I'm not about to do anything to y'all ass," I stated.

"Are y'all gone be alright here alone? I can stay here tonight," Khalil offered.

"Nah, we're good. We need to sit down and talk. There's going to be no fighting," Bri assured him.

"Okay, when do you want to go shopping?" Khalil asked Bri.

"We can go Saturday," she replied back

"Cool, I'm about to go handle some business. I'll call to check on you later," Khalil said before kissing Bri on the forehead.

Joe pulled me into a hug and licked my ear before walking away. Once the guys were out of the door, Bri gave me a strange look. I know she was wondering what's going on. Hell, I don't even know what's going on myself. All I know is that if Joe would have pulled what he just did while we were alone, I'd would have given him some without hesitating.

"Are you going to eat the food that's left or you want something different?" I asked.

"I'm going to eat some noodles. This morning sickness is kicking my ass. Luckily I was sleep while Khalil was here so he didn't notice anything," Bri said low so only I could hear.

"You didn't tell him yet?"

"No, I'm waiting until after Jamaica. That way if his response pisses me off I'd at least got a good vacation out of the trip."

"Okay, well sit down. I can make the noodles for you," I offered.

"You don't have to do that. Plus I need to get my ginger ale and Gatorade from my car."

"I can do that too, now just sit back and relax." I smiled, walking away.

Brielle didn't like people helping and doing things for her. She was so used to doing things on her own. I wasn't there for her like I should've been when we were younger so I just want to make up for that now. I want to be here her entire pregnancy whether Khalil is here for her or not. My job will be to make sure no one is stressing her while she's pregnant. I'm going to find a job out here so that I can help her out, just in case she decides to kick all these bitches out. I want her to know that she don't need nobody.

I went to Bri's car and got her things then went in the kitchen to make her food for her. Just as I was finishing Ryan came down the stairs. She stopped in her tracks when she saw everyone down here as well. Shit was starting to get awkward and weird as hell. Bri must've sensed it because she cleared her throat before speaking.

"Look, things doesn't have to be awkward between all of us. Everybody's emotions were at an all-time high and it was some fucked-up shit that happened. All of y'all paid for Jamaica and I for one plan on enjoying myself and I hope y'all can do the same. Once we get back, we can sit down and discuss everything then take it from there," Bri suggested.

Relief swept across all of their faces. It was like they

planned on Bri telling them that the trip was canceled or that they couldn't go.

"Bri, can I talk to you?" Ryan asked.

"Not if it's about what happened. I'm not willing to discuss that right now because it's only going to piss me off," Bri replied.

The inner me was clapping and cheering my sister on for standing her ground. I'm glad she realizes how fucked up it was for Ryan to play a part in this and didn't buy her sob story. It didn't matter if she wasn't the one that put the drugs in the cup. She actually sat there watching like it was a good idea.

"Alright, at least let me apologize again. I'm sorry for everything and I'll do whatever it takes prove it to you," Ryan stated.

"Me too Bri, I'm sorry," Lena added.

"Yeah, we didn't want you to get hurt. I pop pills all the time," Jayde admitted like that was going to make things okay. Shit, that actually explained a lot about the way she acted.

Bri looked at all three of them for a minute before saying okay and turning her attention back to the TV. I remained silent as I poured Bri's noodles in the bowl. Grabbing a glass from the cabinet, I put ice in it then poured her soda in it. I sat her food on the table and decided to warm up some of the food left over from earlier then sat down to eat with her.

Ryan sat down on the couch while Lena and Jayde left out of the front door. I guess Ryan isn't so buddy-buddy with them now since it's out in the open how fake she is. Little does she know, her not going out with them isn't going to change what I think of her. I'm being patient when it comes to Ryan because she was supposed to be Bri's best friend, but she got one time to look at me wrong and I'm going to knock her in her mouth.

"So, what's going on with you and Joe?" Bri asked, breaking the silence.

"Girl, I don't know. We have sexual chemistry and he seems cool, but I don't know if it's going to go beyond flirting."

"Joe is cool, but I'd suggest being careful because he's still fucking with his baby mama. I'm not sure if it's a relationship but her ass is crazy about him."

"I'm not worried about any of that. I'm not looking for a new relationship right now. I'm just looking for a little bit of fun, if you know what I mean," I laughed.

"Yeah, then you're good," Bri smiled. "Now it's your turn. Everything good between you and KB now?"

"I mean, it's not bad anymore but it's not all the way good either. We still haven't talked about us yet."

"Well from the sounds of it, y'all skipped some steps and went straight to make-up sex," I pointed out.

"Nah, it wasn't no make-up sex. He thought he was going to get some but I told him no so he just wanted to give me head. That I wasn't about to turn down."

"Shit, I know that's right."

Bri and I sat talking for a little while longer before she went up to her room and I went in the office where I sleep. I sat at Bri's desktop and pulled up Indeed so that I could finish putting in job applications. It was time I sat down and started acting like an adult.

CHAPTER FIVE

KHALIL

We've been in Jamaica for a couple days now and everything is going better than expected being that the girls are barely speaking to each other. Bri and Stacey have been spending a lot of time with their brother Mykel. Joe and I tag along with them mostly because Bri never told her family that we aren't together anymore, so it would be strange if I wasn't spending time with her during our birthday trip. Joe's ass is tagging along because he thinks it's going to make Stacey like his ass enough to sleep with him.

I tried warning him that going after Stacey isn't a good idea. That shit can turn bad for all of us if it doesn't work between them. She's my girl's sister and he was fucking with one of her roommates. I don't know where his head is at, but he's a grown man so there's nothing I can do to change his mind. Well, I take that back. I know exactly where his head is. He's thinking with his dick and not his mind. I can't blame him though because Stacey is just as beautiful as her sister, and Bri got me out here doing shit that I've never done before behind a female.

I spent five bands on her when I took her shopping before we got out here and I'm about to take her shopping now just so that I can get some alone time with her. It's like I'm courting her all over again to get her to like me. I told her I'd do whatever it takes to gain her trust. I was the one that fucked up so I can't complain about the hoops she's making me jump through to get her back. I went and got tested like she told me to and gave her the results last week. I just knew after I gave her that paper she was going to break me off. Hell, she could've at least gave me some head to thank me for everything I was doing but she didn't even do that.

I'm trying to do right by her and stay faithful so I've been beating my dick for the past couple weeks. This has been the biggest challenge I've had to experience when it came to a woman. I've never had to beat my dick out of choice and not by force before. Even when women were mad at me they were still fucking because they didn't want me giving the dick to anybody else, but Bri is different. I do know that she better come to her senses soon before I go get some head from another bitch.

We pulled up to The Shoppes at Rose Hall and I found a park. I got out of the car and walked around to the passenger side, helping Bri step out of the car. Surprisingly, she took my hand as we walked toward the entrance. I took that as a good thing because all the other times we were just fronting for everybody. She didn't even allow me to sleep in the bed with her in our room. My ass had been sleeping on the couch. There was an empty bedroom in our villa but it would be hard to explain why me and Bri were sleeping in separate rooms because nobody was crazy enough to think that we weren't having sex.

"You doing alright?" I asked, catching Bri off guard. She

had a weird look on her face. Maybe it was because she barely ate breakfast or lunch earlier.

"Yeah, I'm good. I was just feeling a little light headed," she replied.

"Okay, well we can get food first before we shop if you want," I suggested.

"We can shop first. I'm not hungry right now I just didn't get much sleep last night."

We walked around until we found a Coach store that Bri wanted to go in. I picked this mall because it's known for its luxury stores, designer wear, jewelry, and fragrances. I wanted to make sure that Bri could get some things that she liked as well as me.

Brielle walked around looking at the purses until she came across a pink bag, shoes, and sunglasses that she liked. She was satisfied with the items that she chose so we went to check out. The total was a thousand dollars. I took my debit card from my wallet and handed it to the sales lady. She had a look of surprise on her face that I was the one paying and not Bri herself.

The lady handed Bri the bag and we thanked her before leaving the store. We did some more shopping until Bri started complaining about her feet hurting. By the time we finished shopping and grabbing something to eat it was almost nine o'clock when we made it to the house. We had been out for damn near six hours. It didn't seem like it was that long though. I guess it had to do with me being happy that I had got Bri all to myself.

When we walked in the house, Stacey, Malik, and Joe were sitting down on the couch.

"Hey, you two are just in time. We were about to watch a movie. Do y'all want to join us?" Stacey asked, looking up at us.

I wanted to be selfish and yell no. I wasn't ready to go back to reality and share Bri. Today felt like old times between us. It made me realize how much I missed her. If I could help it, I'll never do anything again that would jeopardize her leaving me. I know it hasn't even been a year yet since we've been together and I already know that I'm going to marry her one day. If I thought she'd tell me yes right now, I'd go to the jewelers and buy her a big ass rock that I'm sure she'd hate because she doesn't like flashy things.

"Yeah, we'll watch a movie with y'all. Just let us go put our bags away," Bri answered for both of us.

Joe had a dumb ass smirk on his face because he knew I didn't want to watch no damn movie. I'd rather be making a movie, but I'm just going to go with the flow and follow Bri's lead. It's her world now and I just live in it.

We walked in the bedroom and Bri dropped her bags on the floor.

"Did you enjoy yourself today?" I asked, looking at all of her bags.

"Yeah, I did, thank you for everything." She smiled before kissing me on the cheek.

"I had a good time as always. You know I love being able to spend time with you alone," I reminded her.

Bri stood staring in my eyes and it was the same look of lust that I had. It was like she wanted me and was waiting for me to make the first move. I leaned in to kiss her on the lips just as Stacey started calling our names. They had found a movie and were ready to start it.

I cursed under my breath as I followed Bri out of the room. They ass sure knew how to fuck up a wet dream. Since the couch was full I sat down in the love seat and pulled Bri down on my lap. Instead of protesting, she leaned back and cuddled up under me.

We sat and watched some movie called *The Black Phone*. It

was a decent movie but I was glad that it was finally over. Having Bri sitting on my lap like this was torturous.

Once the movie was over me and Bri got up and headed to the bedroom while everybody else did whatever it was they were going to do. Walking in the bedroom, I sat on the bed pulling Bri on top of me. I placed kisses on her neck that led up to her lips. She met my lips then slid her tongue in my mouth. We sat making out like a couple of high school kids.

Brielle was panting and squeezing her thighs around me as I ran my fingers through her hair and all over her body. She was hot and ready like a Lil' Caesar's pizza. She broke away from the kiss and stood from my lap, leaving me to feel lonely. I wanted to pull her back down but instead, she grabbed me by the hand and pulled me up from the bed.

She held my hand and led the way to our adjoined bathroom. No matter where I go I make sure to have my own bathroom for these purposes. I can spend as much time in there as I want with no one interrupting me.

We stripped out of our clothes then turned on the water and climbed in the shower. Bri wrapped one of her arms around my neck and used her free hand to stroke my dick.

"Bri, if you don't stop now I won't be able to control myself," I warned her. She responded by moving her hand faster. I looked into her eyes and kissed her deeply. The kiss was getting rough and nasty quick.

I lifted Bri up, causing her to wrap her arms around my neck and legs around my waist. I slid her down on my dick, causing us both to moan. She was wet as hell and her pussy was gripping my dick like a too-little glove. I missed the hell out of her. I was a damn fool to fuck this up. Moving in and out of her felt good as hell. She will always be the best I've ever had.

Sliding out of her, I turned her around and entered her

from the back.

"Ahhhh shit, Khalil, I'm about to cum," she screamed as I picked up the speed.

I went faster, using one hand to hold her waist and the other hand holding onto the back her neck. Her screams and moans filling the bathroom had me ready to bust quick. Biting onto her shoulder, I felt her tighten around me until her juices started squirting down my dick.

She might have thought I was done with her but I was nowhere near it. I was about to remind her what she had been missing out on.

Pulling out of her, I grabbed her hand and led the way back to the bed. I laid down and she knew what time it was. She slid down on my dick and I held her waist as she rode me. I knew she missed us just as much as I did.

"Fuck baby," I moaned, not being able to control myself anymore.

She leaned down, kissing my neck making my dick jump to the beat of her drum. Her pussy was so good that I didn't even realize I was cumming until she slid all the way up the tip and back down, covering it. Her pussy was dangerous as hell. I'd go broke behind her ass.

"Oh my god, I'm cumming Khalil," she yelled as she tried to slow down the pace, but it was too late because I had already started cumming so I was about to finish shooting up the club.

"Damn Bri, I think you about to have my baby now," I announced as I busted the hardest nut I have in a long time.

"It's too late for that," she replied, climbing off of me.

I brushed off what she said and went into the bathroom to get a towel. I wet it with soap and water, cleaning myself off. Then I grabbed another towel, doing the same thing, taking it out to clean Bri. After she was clean I put the towel back then climbed in bed next to her. She was unusually quiet and had me thinking that she regretted what just happened. Maybe it had to do with me saying she was going to have my baby. I was only semi joking though. I wouldn't mind her having my baby, because then that meant she wasn't going anywhere, but I know she's in school and has other goals before we get to that point.

"Why are you so quiet? I was only joking about the baby thing. I can go get you a plan B in the morning if you want me to," I offered.

"That won't be necessary," she replied, turning to look at me.

"Why? You went and got on birth control without telling me?"

"No, it's not that either. When I went to the hospital the night after the club I found out that I was five weeks pregnant," she admitted.

I stood from the bed and grabbed a pair of boxers to put on while I allowed what she had just said to register.

"So you've known you was pregnant for almost a month now and you didn't tell me? When were you going to tell me, or did you plan on killing my seed and not letting me know?" I wasn't mad about her being pregnant. I was mad that she was keeping shit from me. I know I fucked up, but this is a child that we're talking about.

"Honestly, at first I didn't know what I was going to do. It was so much going on all at once and we weren't on good terms. I wasn't going to make a decision without discussing things with you first. I was going to tell you about the baby when we made it back to Chicago to discuss our relationship."

"Well I don't want to wait until we get back to discuss us or the baby. Let me take you to dinner tomorrow and we can put everything out in the open," I suggested.

Bri hesitated before agreeing to let me take her out. So now not only was I going to have to convince her to make things official with me again, but now I was going to have to convince her to keep our baby. She's the only woman that I've been with that I was willing to have a baby with. I can't wait to tell my parents. I know my mother will be happy as hell because in her mind she was never going to become a grandmother.

I laid down in bed and pulled Bri close to me, kissing her on the forehead. I couldn't believe that she was carrying my baby. I waited until she was sleep before climbing out of bed. I put on a pair of basketball shorts then grabbed my blunt and left the room. I walked outside on the patio where Stacey and Joe were kissing and feeling on each other. If I walked out a few minutes later I probably would've walked in on them fucking. It's only a matter of time before it happens, so they might as well get it over with and out of their system.

"If y'all about to fuck, go inside because I need to smoke," I said, getting their attention.

"Nigga, where you come from? Let me find out Bri still ain't gave your cranky ass none," Joe replied.

I ignored him and got back to smoking my blunt. Stacey whispered something to Joe before getting up to walk away. He smacked her on the ass as she walked away.

"She let you hit?" I asked once she was out of earshot.

"Man nah, I was close just now until your cock blocking ass came out here. Why you ain't in bed with your girl? If you stayed still maybe she'd give you some."

"Don't worry about my dick or my girl. I just put her ass to sleep. I had to come out for a minute to clear my head."

"Why? What's going on? Did something happen?"

I thought about whether I should tell Joe about the baby yet because I didn't know if Bri was going to keep it. I could use some advice though so I decided to tell him.

"I just found out Bri is pregnant, but don't say shit. We're going to sit down and talk about everything tomorrow."

"How do you feel about knowing that?" he asked, not seeming to be surprised by the news.

"You already knew didn't you?"

"Yeah, I walked in on her and Stacey talking about it last week. I told her to tell you and she said she was waiting for the right time."

"Man, how could you keep something like that from me?"

"You're my brother and I look at Bri as a sister. If y'all are going to be together she needs to be able to trust me as well. Anything can happen living the lifestyle we live so I need her to know that I'll be there for her."

"You're right man, thank you for looking out for her. Do you think she's going to keep it?"

"She's going to keep it. She didn't tell you because she didn't know how you would react, so she at least wanted to be able to enjoy her birthday first in case you didn't want the baby."

"How could she think I wouldn't want her to have my baby after everything we been through? I wasn't strapping up or pulling out every time we had sex so I knew the consequences."

"It's because of what y'all been through that had her nervous. You have to reassure her that you're going to be there for her and the baby whether y'all are together or not. She's scared right now. You have to remember that the last time she was pregnant her boyfriend died during that time and you cheated on her. She's been stressed out enough so now you need to make it easier for her."

For once Joe was actually giving good advice. I'm glad that he and Bri have the kind of bond that they have because he was right about the lifestyle that we lived. Anything could happen to either one of us. We could end up dead or in jail so I'll be comfortable knowing that she has him to look out for her or our child if anything happened to me.

We stood outside and talked until the blunt was done then we went back in the house, going our separate ways. I went inside of the room and took my clothes off then climbed in bed next to Bri, pulling her close to me. She was right back in my arms where she belonged. I fell asleep with a smile on my face for the first time in a long time.

CHAPTER SIX
BRIELLE

Last night ended on a good note and this morning started on a better one. I woke up to Khalil devouring my pussy then giving me slow back shots. I didn't know what I missed more, him or his sex game. Sex was definitely doing my body good. I was already feeling better compared to how I had been feeling. My morning sickness was also under control and I was more than thankful for that.

I spent the day with Stacey and Mykel. We went out to lunch and went to a few shops to get souvenirs. I loved being able to spend time with my siblings, especially Mykel because it had been a while since we hung out. I tried to convince my parents to come with us but all they wanted to do was sit by the pool and drink. That didn't surprise me one bit though. I'm just glad that they've been able to control their liquor so far and were being respectful to Khalil's family.

As much as I enjoyed spending time with my siblings, I was looking forward to dinner with Khalil. I was glad that he was invested in making things right between us. Also, from his reaction I'm sure that meant that he wanted to have this baby with me. I was going to remind him that he didn't have to be there if he didn't want to though. I had money saved and I could always pick up a better job than tutoring in order to support my baby.

Looking in the mirror, I checked myself out to make sure that my look was giving what it was supposed to. I wanted a sexy but chic kind of look, so I put on a black, short, spaghetti-strapped skater dress and a pair of silver gladiator sandals. The dress only went down a couple inches to my thighs so there was no bending over for me, and hopefully the wind doesn't blow or I'll be getting my Marilyn Monroe on.

"You're ready to go?" Khalil asked, stepping behind me.

"Yeah," I said, turning around to look at him. He looked good as hell in his black slacks and white button-up shirt. His shirt looked like it was tailored just for him. His biceps were popping and all I could think about was holding onto his strong arms while bouncing up and down on his dick. I had to hurry up and shake those thoughts away or we'd never make it out of this bedroom.

"You look beautiful as always," he complimented, roaming his eyes over me. No matter how many times this man has seen me naked he still makes me nervous and makes me feel like the most beautiful woman in the world.

"Thanks baby," I replied before kissing him on the lips.

I grabbed my purse then we left out of the room. We told everybody goodbye that was sitting in the living room then we left out of the house. Usually Khalil would drive us but today we were using one of his father's drivers. I didn't know the reason but I wasn't complaining because it didn't affect me.

We climbed in back of the town car and headed to the restaurant. About thirty minutes passed when we pulled up to Cru Bar & Grill. We got out of the car and Khalil led the way inside. He gave the hostess his name then we were escorted upstairs to the rooftop. Typically I don't enjoy eating outside, but the scenery made this so much better. There was reggae music playing and some people were up out of their seats dancing and drinking.

We sat down in the back where we were able to see everything going on around us.

"Good evening, I'm Kenisha and I'll be your waitress for the day. Can I start you off with something to drink?" she asked.

"I'll have a Hennessy VSOP," Khalil answered.

"You can get me a bottle of water and a white sangria," I replied.

"Are you two ready to order as well?"

"Not at the moment. We're still looking," Khalil told her.

"Okay, take your time. I'm going to put in your drink orders," she said, walking away.

"Why did you order that sangria? You're not allowed to drink while pregnant," Khalil told me.

"It's fine, I'm allowed to have a glass of wine plus this is mixed with lime, lemon juice, pineapple juice, and ginger ale."

"Alright, but that's the only one you're drinking."

"Whatever you say daddy," I replied sarcastically.

"Girl, you better stop playing before we don't make it to have dinner."

"Don't threaten me with a good time." I smirked.

"Oh, you ain't have enough from last night and this morning, I see. Don't worry, I'll have you calling me daddy when we get back tonight."

I was about to respond but the waitress came over with our drinks, interrupting our flirtatious conversation.

She handed us our drinks and we gave her our dinner orders. She took the orders and was gone as quick as she had come.

"Why do you keep staring at me? Do I have something on my face?" I asked curiously.

"No, you don't have anything on your face. I'm just taking in your beauty. I'm one lucky man to have you in my life."

"I'm glad that you're finally realizing how lucky you are."

"I'm not just realizing anything, Bri. I've always known how lucky I am. Me sleeping with Krystal didn't have anything to do with how I felt about you. You've always been perfect for me. You're beautiful with a dope ass personality and your sex game is A1. I was just being dumb as hell and in my feelings."

It felt good hearing those things from Khalil but I still had unanswered questions. I needed clarification on a few things before I went all in again for another round.

"Since we're on the subject of feelings, do you still have them for Krystal? Is that why you picked her to sleep with? I know you have other women that you could have used to get your dick wet."

Khalil sighed for a minute before answering. I'm guessing he was thinking about how to answer my question without making things worse.

"I don't have feelings for Krystal anymore. I barely had feelings left for her when I started talking to you. She was just a convenient person to go see. I cut her off a long time ago. That was the first time that I had seen her since we got together. I really did want to do things right with you because I love you," he confessed as the waitress came over with our food.

I waited for the waitress to sit our food down. When she was out of earshot we picked up our conversation.

"How do I know the next time you get mad or times get hard between us you won't go out and sleep with her or another woman?"

"I'm telling you now that I fucked up and I know that trust doesn't happen overnight. Like I've been telling you, I'm willing to do whatever it takes to get that trust back, even if it means going to counseling. I want to be there for you as well as our baby if you plan on keeping it."

"I am going to keep it. I couldn't bring myself to get rid of the baby whether you're here or not. I appreciate you saying you will be here, but I don't want you to feel like you're obligated to stick around. Neither one of us planned this so I'm giving you a way out now," I said, eating a spoonful of my mashed potatoes and salmon.

"I don't need a way out. I knew there was a possibility of you getting pregnant when I stopped using condoms. It wasn't like you tricked me and made me think you were on birth control. I knew that you weren't and I still nutted in you."

"All of that sounds good Khalil and I want to trust you. Without trust our relationship will never have a solid foundation. You need to show me respect and not have me out here looking crazy in front of other bitches. I should be the only woman that should be getting pleasured from you. No other woman should be able to throw shit else in my face. Do you know how embarrassing it was to find out what you did from Jayde? She couldn't wait to throw that shit in my face."

"I know and I own up to all of it. You don't have to worry about that happening again. I'm going to do right by you and our child. I'm going to show you that I can be the man that you fell in love with," he assured me.

I was happy to hear that we were on the same page. I wanted things to work for us. If not for me, at least for our unborn child. I'm not naive enough to just take Khalil's word. He has to have to show me that he can be the man I need him to be. I was a firm believer in action speaking louder than words.

We continued talking about us and our future over dinner. Once we were done Khalil paid the check then we left the restaurant. Instead of going home we went to the beach. I took my shoes off then we went for a walk along the shoreline. The breeze felt good as hell. Khalil walked behind me, walking with his hand on my waist to make sure my dress didn't fly up.

We walked and talked for almost an hour before we headed home. When we got there it was only Khalil's parents sitting in the living room. Everyone else was out and about. We talked to them for a few minutes before going to our room. As soon as the door was closed Khalil was all over me.

"Khalil, wait, your parents are woke and down the hall. You don't know how to be quiet," I pointed out.

"Brielle, don't act like you be quiet."

"I'm not, that's why I'm saying we should wait."

"I don't want to wait. I'll be quiet, I promise."

Before I could respond he was lifting my dress and sliding my panties to the side. Once he started massaging my clit there was no protest left in my body. I laid down on the bed and allowed my baby to handle his business.

CHAPTER SEVEN
JOE

We were bored sitting around the house so we decided to go to the bonfire on the beach. It started off as me, Mykel, and Stacey. Then when I looked up Ryan, Jayde, and Lena were out here as well. I could tell Ryan had a thing for Mykel from her body language. He didn't seem to pay much attention to her. I didn't know if it was because she was Bri's friend or he just wasn't interested.

Stacey and I were standing around talking until some Reggae song came on. She started twirling her hips before bending over twerking her ass. She had on a pair of blue jean shorts that were barely holding her ass cheeks. She was leaving very little for the imagination.

I couldn't resist feeling her ass against me so I walked behind her and held onto her waist as she threw her ass back. She could definitely twerk but now she had me wondering if she knew how to do this on a dick. She turned her head and looked back at me while placing her hands on her knees, dancing even harder. I know I smiling like a damn fool. She was starting to make my manhood stand at attention, which caused her to slow down and grind on my shit. At this point she was playing crack-head games. She knew what she was doing and she was enjoying every bit of it. Since she wanted to play, I was going to play along with her. I held onto her waist and started pushing her back and forth like she was getting hit from the back.

We danced on each other for two more songs until I couldn't take anymore. She had me ready to take them lil' ass shorts off and give her all this dick I had to offer.

I looked in the cooler that we brought out and pulled out the bottle of Patrón. I took out the shot glasses as well, pouring us both one. She took the drink from me and knocked it back. One shot turned into two and two turned into three. Before we realized it the bottle was empty and we were both tipsy as hell. We should've stopped after shot number three because it was a good fifteen-minute walk back to the villa.

"Come walk me back. I have to pee," Stacey whined.

"Ain't nobody tell you to drink all that alcohol and cranberry juice," I replied.

"You're the one that kept giving it to me. If I ain't know no better I'd think you were trying to get me drunk so that you could get in my pants."

"Baby, we both know I didn't have to get you drunk for that. You been begging for me to take that lil' pussy."

"Nah my nigga, this pussy fat as hell. Ain't shit little over here." She smirked before walking away.

I was just talking shit. I knew her pussy was fat from when I was playing all up in it last night. I was ready to slide up in her out there on the patio when KB came walking out on us. I sat talking to him so long that by the time I went back in I had missed my beat. She was already in her room sleep with the door locked.

I followed behind her because I wasn't about to let her

walk back by herself dressed the way she was. She was asking for somebody to snatch her thick ass up. She had on those little ass shorts with a bikini top and a pair of slides. She was dressed for the beach even though she had no intention on getting in the water.

We talked while we walked back to the house. When we made it inside, the living room was empty so that meant our parents were in their rooms. We made our way up the stairs and I could hear Bri and KB talking. I figured they were back and just wanted to spend time alone rather than come with the group. I was happy that they were able to get it together. I liked Brielle for my brother. In the short amount of time that she's been in his life she's kept him grounded. I never did like him with Krystal. It didn't matter that she was Kenya's sister. That's the only reason I did put up with her ass. Hell, at this point, the only reason I put up with Kenya is because of our daughter. As more time goes by I realize that she's not for me. I'm finally starting to see what KB was telling me all along.

Instead of going into the bathroom Stacey went into her bedroom. I was confused because she was just acting like she couldn't hold her pee. A couple minutes later she came out of the room with clothes in her hand.

"Why you standing outside the bathroom like a creep?" she asked.

"I was trying to let your ass go in first since you had to use it so bad."

"Oh, well I'm about to shower so you can go in first," she offered.

"You can go in. I'll use the one downstairs because I need to get some water anyway," I told her before walking away.

I headed down the stairs and went to the bathroom. Once I finished handling my business I went in the refrigerator and grabbed a couple bottles of water from the refrigerator. Going back upstairs, I went in my room and grabbed a pair of boxers then went inside one of the other bathrooms to take a quick shower. After I was done I went to my room and laid down in bed.

I laid there staring for a minute but I wasn't tired, so I knew sleep wasn't going to find me no time soon. My dick was hard and I tried putting my mind somewhere else, but all I could think about was Stacey. I laid there for another fifteen minutes then said fuck it. I was about to see if Stacey was all talk or if she was actually ready to get down.

Climbing out of the bed, I reached in my suitcase and pulled out the box of Magnums I brought on the trip just in case. I knew I was going to get some from somebody at some point I just didn't know who. Jayde had been trying to make her way to my bed every night since we been here but I wasn't going. I was trying to hold out for Stacey. Now if she don't give me none then I might just have Jayde give me some head.

Walking out of my room, I walked across the hall to Stacey's room. I turned the knob and was surprised that it was unlocked. Usually she locks it behind her when she's going to bed.

Walking in her room, I locked the door as I appeared in her sight, causing her to jump. She was sitting on the edge of the bed moisturizing her body.

"Knock much?" she asked, looking up at me casually like she wasn't but ass naked. She was confident about her body and she had every right to be. She looked just as good with her clothes off as she does with them on.

"Girl, we both know you were waiting on me or you would've locked the door. It don't make no sense how sexy you are," I told her, walking over to her.

I took my boxers off then pushed her back on the bed and opened her legs. I rubbed her mound a little before separating her lips. Rubbing between them, I felt her wetness soaking my fingers. I slipped one finger in her and started stroking her pussy. She started moaning like crazy and I was ready to taste her.

I laid down on the bed and positioned her so that she could ride my face. I was a skinny nigga but I know how to hold my breath under water.

I sucked on her clit nice and slow. Then I started to fuck her pussy with my tongue. She started bucking on it and riding it up and down.

"Baby, I'm 'bout to cum," Stacey moaned while riding my face harder. I licked her pussy lips and stuck my tongue in and out of her pussy. Then I went back to her clit and sucked it firm and slow.

"Fuckkkk," she moaned as she creamed all over my face. I tried to lick up every drop. I licked her pussy clean as she whimpered in orgasmic bliss. She had some of the best pussy I ever tasted.

I slid her down from my face and positioned her right on my dick. I pushed my dick up in her tight walls. As wet as she was I still had to fight a little to get in.

"You better not get attached," she told me as she slid up and down my dick.

"Attached? Hoes want me, not the other way around," I reminded her.

"That's the thing, I'm not like the hoes you're used to fucking," she pointed out and picked up the pace some, making my stomach knot up.

"Fuck, Stacey," I groaned.

She was talking about attached and it was feeling like I was already addicted to her pussy. She leaned down kissing on my neck, making my dick jump.

"Arrghhh," she semi screamed as she finally took all of me

in. I couldn't handle her riding me like this. She had me feeling like a bitch.

I flipped her over doggy style, making her put a deep arch in her back keeping her ass up. I had been wanting her in this position since the day I met her.

Sticking my dick back into her warm pussy, she contracted her muscles around it. She was getting nothing but dick from this position.

"Yo, stop doing that," I groaned, trying to make her loosen her grip before she made me cum quick.

"Joe, wait," she protested as I stroked her leaking pussy. She was running like a faucet. I made sure to fill her up with all ten inches.

She kept trying to push me away so I pinned her arms behind her back, speeding up.

"Fuck, Stacey, your pussy good as hell," I groaned, pounding her while I bit my bottom lip.

"I'm about to cummmmm," she started screaming loud, so I pushed her head into the pillow before she woke up the entire house.

"See, this what happens when you make me wait. This my pussy now," I boasted, slapping her on the ass.

Moments later she gave in, cumming again. I stroked her a little more before pulling out, busting on her ass. So much for using the condoms I bought. I fell on the bed trying to catch my breath. I was too tired to go shower but I was sticky as hell.

I laid there for a few minutes before getting up and pulling her along with me. I was starting to regret not getting one of the rooms that had a bathroom in it.

Stacey got up from the bed, putting her robe on. Once she was covered I got up, putting my boxers back on, then we left the room to go shower. What was supposed to be a quick shower turned into us fucking for another twenty minutes. I was glad that it was only Bri and Khalil's room on this side of the house because we were loud as hell. I know they're going to talk shit when we wake up in the morning, but it was definitely worth it.

Since we had wet up her bed we went inside my room to sleep instead. Normally I wouldn't care about her bed being wet and I would've made her sleep by herself, but she was different. She was sexy as hell and could take dick. If she knew how to suck it just as well, she was being moved to the top of my list. I was serious when I told her that she belonged to me now. She wasn't about to put it on me like this then act like nothing happened.

CHAPTER EIGHT
STACEY

The following morning I woke up on cloud nine. I could see why Jayde was acting crazy over Joe's ass. He had some of the best dick I've ever had in my life, and I'm not exaggerating. Don't get me wrong now, I've had some good dick before but nothing like his. His shit was lethal and I was going to have to be careful with him. I can't have him out here having me look crazy.

I sat up in bed and came face to face to Joe's hard dick. He grabbed me by my jaw and I opened my mouth, allowing him to enter it. I started moving my head back and forth at a slow pace. He bit his lip when I stuck out my tongue. Eventually I started deep throating his dick. My gag reflex was on one hundred.

He held onto the back of head, making me pick up the pace and causing slob to drip down my chin.

"Hmmm shit," he groaned as I twirled my tongue from side to side. He was starting to shake and quiver at my touch.

I stopped sucking his dick and started jacking it as I sucked on his nut sack. I transitioned from sucking his balls to sucking on the tip of his dick, making it jump.

"Fuck, don't move," he groaned as he started to fuck my throat. I was taking it all like the pro that I was. I belonged in the hall of fame for my head game.

"I'm about to nut," he announced, causing me to suck harder. His eyes were rolling to the back of his head as he dropped his load down my throat. I swallowed every drop before slowly releasing him from my mouth until I got back to the tip. I had his ass jumping and pushing my head away. "Stop that shit Stacey, my dick numb as hell," he said, causing me to laugh. Niggas always wanted to keep sucking on your pussy after you cum but they can't handle you sucking on they dick after they nut.

I got up from the bed and put my robe on. It was already eleven and I needed to freshen up so that I could get my day started.

I left Joe's room and went inside the bathroom. As I was closing the door Joe appeared. I stepped all the way inside and allowed him to come in. I told his ass not to get attached, now he was following me around. This is why I don't sleep with everybody because they don't know how to handle a bitch with good pussy.

I took the towel from the towel rack and handed it to him while I used the other one to wash my face. Once I was done with that I brushed my teeth then climbed in the shower. Joe brushed his teeth then joined me. I knew he wasn't here just to shower so I lifted my leg onto the tub, providing access to my kitty. He filled me up, instantly causing a moan to escape my lips. I don't think I'll ever be able to get used to his size. After today, I was going to have to ration the pussy for him if I wanted to keep my walls intact.

We finished up our session in the shower then we washed

each other up before climbing out. I wrapped a towel around me and went inside of my bedroom, locking the door this time. I didn't want to give Joe any bright ideas. He had my honey pot sore as hell. I was about to be walking around funny all day because of his ass.

I dried off then moisturized my body. Today was just going to be a chill day at the beach so I put on my black bikini with a pair of black shorts and some pink slides. My hair was a mess and I didn't feel like straightening it due to the humidity, so I pulled it back into a ponytail.

Once I was done I headed downstairs to the dining room where Ryan, Jayde, Bri, and Mykel were sitting down eating. I walked over and sat at the table next to Bri.

There were eggs, waffles, sausage, bacon, breakfast potatoes, orange juice, and apple juice on the table. I put a little bit of it all on my plate and poured a cup of orange juice.

"Hey girl hey, how was your night?" Bri asked, already knowing the answer.

"Shit, from what it sounded like, just as good as yours." I smiled, thinking about last night and this morning.

"Aye, I know y'all see me sitting here," Mykel said, jumping in our conversation.

"Boy bye, you know we ain't virgins," I replied.

"As far as I'm concerned, both of my lil' sisters are virgins until they get married," Mykel stated.

"Shit, the chances of that is long gone, big bro. I hate to break it to you," I laughed.

Mykel shook his head before going back to eating his food. I loved getting under his skin because to him we were still little girls who needed him to fight our battles.

I was halfway done with my food when Joe came walking in dressed and looking refreshed. He spoke to everybody but kept his eyes on me. If everybody didn't know we fucked before, they know now. This nigga was obvious as hell.

"Bri, where KB at?" Joe inquired.

"When I left him he was in bed sleeping like a newborn baby. You can call me melatonin," she beamed.

"Really Bri? What the hell is wrong with you and Stacey today?" Mykel asked, irritated. We were actually getting under his skin and I was loving every bit of it.

"What? I'm just saying. There's nothing wrong with me. I'm like Tony the Tiger. I'm greatttt," Bri laughed, causing everybody to laugh with her except Jayde. She was sitting there like a stick in the mud. I'm sure she's in her feelings about Joe, but it is what it is. He ain't my man nor are we dating. He was just a means to an end. I was horny and he was willing to give out the dick.

"Joe, did you have sex with her?" Jayde blurted, catching us off guard.

"What?" Joe asked, confused.

"You heard me. Did you fuck her? Because if you did that's foul as hell since we all live under the same roof," she replied.

"For now," I added. I wanted to remind her that she may be homeless once this trip is over so mind her manners.

"Jayde, don't ask me no shit like that. I don't keep up with what you doing with your body so don't keep track of my dick. It ain't your business if I slept with her or not. It's not like you two are friends, so it's open season," he said, sitting down across from me.

I liked how politically correct he was regarding the situation. It wasn't nobody's business what we had going on, especially hers.

Jayde looked like she wanted to say something, but instead she remained quiet. I guess she was trying to think of a response to what he had just said but apparently she didn't have one.

I finished eating my food then went to put me and Bri's dishes in the sink. I made a mental note to ask her about her morning sickness. It seemed like she was able to eat real food while out here.

I finished washing our dishes then went back to the dining room to see when Bri would be ready to go to the beach. I ducked my head in and could see that it was only Jayde and Joe in there. They were talking amongst themselves lowly so I couldn't really hear what they were saying until she got loud. I stayed peeking in so I could see what they were talking about. It's not so much that I care about their conversation but more or so that I'm nosey like that.

"Just answer the question, Joe. Did you have sex with that girl?" she yelled.

"I told your ass to stop asking me that. What does it matter if I did? What's it going to change for you? I don't fuck with you like that no more," he stated.

"It doesn't matter, you know the situation between all of us. That's some messy shit to deal with her. You know how I feel about you," Jayde whined.

"Just stop Jayde, there was never going to be a relationship between me and you. We were just having fun," he replied.

"Okay, so what is it for you and Stacey? She's just another notch under your belt?"

"You're starting to piss me off now. I told you to leave it alone because I didn't want to hurt your feelings."

"Oh, so you like her huh?"

Joe took a deep breath before finally speaking.

"Look, I would never be in a relationship with a girl like you. It was fun to get my dick sucked but that was about the only thing you had going. Your pussy is trash and so is your personality, now leave me the fuck alone," he yelled.

I stood there almost feeling bad for Jayde because that was harsh. She asked for it though, because he told her to stop asking him. I made a mental note not to get on his bad side, because if he talked to me like that I'll punch his ass.

"Is that really how you feel?" she asked stupidly, sounding like she was about to cry. She was just plain ol' pitiful at this point. How a man tell you that not only are you trash but also your punany and you still sit there and try to talk to him. Get some dignity or a backbone or something. I know the dick good, but not disrespect and no self-respect kind of good.

Joe looked at her for a minute then got up from the table, taking his plate with him. It was a shame that he couldn't even enjoy his food in peace. As long as she didn't say anything to me about the situation I was good. She could get on his nerves as long as she wants.

I hurriedly walked back in the kitchen so that Joe couldn't see I was eavesdropping. I opened the refrigerator and bent over to get a bottle of water when I felt a presence behind me. I knew it wasn't nobody but Joe so I started to fuck with him. I stood up, making sure I rubbed my ass across him the whole time.

Grabbing me by wrist, he spun me around and pushed my back up against the counter. Instinctively, my arms wrapped around his neck. He leaned down and nuzzled his nose into my neck, inhaling my scent before smelling it. He placed soft kisses on my neck then made his way to my lips where I welcomed the kiss. Typically I don't kiss guys I'm not in a relationship with, but I can't resist Joe's succulent lips. The lips that did wonders to my body last night.

We were standing there in the kitchen kissing, and I swear I was getting hot and bothered. His hand started roaming over my body and fucking with him, I was going to have to change my bikini bottoms.

"You kissing me like you wish you was kissing my other lips again," I flirted, breaking the kiss.

"Shitttt, if you want me to I can. We can go upstairs right now and I'll eat your shit until you pass out." He smirked but I knew he was serious.

"Nah, because if we go up to that room right now we both know we'll miss going to the beach and I told my sister I'll go with her, but once that's over I'm all yours," I told him before leaning in to kiss him again.

"Really Joe? I thought you didn't kiss or give head, but you in here making plans to do so with this bitch?" Jayde asked, showing up out of nowhere. I'm guessing she was standing at the doorway

"Girl, who you calling a bitch? Whatever happened or didn't happen between y'all doesn't have anything to do with me so keep me out of y'all shit," I told her.

"It has everything to do with you. Everything was good between us until you came in the picture," she said.

"If everything was good between y'all he wouldn't have came chasing me, and from what he told me y'all don't even fuck around anymore. It's not like you two were in a relationship together, so he's free game." I shrugged.

"Jayde, my parents are here and so are hers, so chill out with this disrespectful shit. You being loud for no reason," Joe said, making her madder.

"I'm the one being disrespectful? You're parading this bitch around like we didn't just fuck last week. We both know you'll be calling me when we make it back home." She smirked.

I stepped from around Joe and walked in Jayde's face.

"You got one more time to call me a bitch and I'm going to drag your ass through this house by your nappy ass ponytail.

Don't think his parents being here will save you. I don't tolerate disrespect from nobody. I been trying to keep it cool since it's my sister's birthday trip, but don't get it twisted," I warned her.

"Stacey, get out of her face and leave her alone. You know better than to be arguing over a man," Mykel said, walking over to me. He wasn't there at first so that meant we were loud and he could hear us from the other room.

"No, let's get something straight. I'm not arguing over Joe because I know men gone be men. I'm putting her in her place for disrespecting me. I was trying to do the right thing and mind my business. I haven't said anything to this girl none while I was here but everybody want to act like she's innocent and I'm a bully.

"I never called you a bully. All I'm saying is calm down. It's not worth it. You're going to have high blood pressure at a young age with your temper," Mykel pointed out.

"Like I said, if she mind her business everything will be good. I'm not Bri, I'm Stacey. She's the one that's always the bigger person. That trait skipped me."

"Well maybe you need to let it come back around. You don't always have to be defensive and it's okay to walk away," he told me.

I hated how lame my brother could be now that he's older. He's always trying to be the peacemaker. He has Bri beat in that category. At least she stands up for herself.

"You're wasting your breath right now Mykel, because I don't plan on changing no time soon. Actually, I guess you can say I am changing, because had this been somewhere else you would be in here picking Jayde up off this floor. I wouldn't have warned her," I said, walking away. I no longer wanted to be a part of this conversation. At this point I was over everybody except my sister, so I went upstairs to her room to find her.

I knocked on the door and waited for her answer.

"Who is it?" she called out.

"Me," I replied.

I heard shuffling before KB opened the bedroom door. He was standing there in a pair of black swim trunks and a wife heater. I couldn't help but admire his physique. My sister definitely hit the jackpot with him. He's sexy, has money, and is willing to take care of her. She's going to have to learn how to pick her battles when dealing with a man like him.

"Hey, is Joe downstairs or in his room?" KB asked.

"Why you asking me? I'm not your brother's keeper," I answered.

"Yo chill, it's not about you being his keeper. I was just asking a question because Bri told me y'all was downstairs eating. You standing here acting like you in your feelings or something. You good?" KB inquired.

"My bad, I'm just irritated right now. He was down in the kitchen when I left."

"Cool," he told me before turning his attention to Bri. "I'm about to go see what's up with Joe. When you ready to go come down," he said before kissing her on the lips.

Once he was gone I closed the room door and flopped down on the bed and told Bri everything that just happened.

"Maybe I should stop talking to him now. I don't do this back-and-forth shit over niggas," I stated.

"You already knew the chances of this happening before you slept with him and you said that you didn't care. It's just fun right? So I say do you. Don't cut things off with him because of her bitter ass. End things when you're ready," she told me, making perfectly good sense. I did know the consequences of getting involved with Joe. I'm not worried about Jayde and I'm not about to allow her to get in my way.

We laid there and continued having girl talk. She told me

all about her date last night and I was happy for her. She deserved all the happiness this world had to offer. She was dealt a bad hand her last relationship and was lucky enough to find KB the second go around.

Once we were done talking Bri got dressed in a white bathing suit with the sides cut out and a pair of blue jeans shorts with white slides. She pulled her hair up into a bun and put on a pair of white Coach glasses. My niece or nephew was doing her body good because she had the pregnancy glow going on.

Bri grabbed her purse then we left the room. I stopped in my room to get my purse and sunglasses then we headed down the stairs where Ryan, Mykel, Joe, and KB were waiting on us. This situation was kind of weird. I didn't know what was going on with Ryan. She was like the odd person out on this trip. Jayde and Lena hung out with others while Ryan tagged along wherever we went. The odd part about it was that all she did was speak to us but never tried to hold a conversation. It was like she was letting her presence be known that she was there for Bri without actually being there. I can't deal with all this weird shit but it is what is. Like I said before, if I was Bri I'd kick all they asses out, but being that I know Bri the way she is, she's probably not going to do that. Well, I put it this way, she's not going to put her raggedy best friend out without having nowhere to go. She'll most likely give Jayde and Lena a notice, which is too nice if you ask me. They have more options though than Ryan since they're students. They have the option to stay in dorms or campus housing.

We left the house and went to the beach outside the villa instead of down by where the bonfire was. I took the blankets from the bag Joe was carrying and spread them out. Bri took off her shorts and laid down on the blanket with KB lying next to her. I wanted to go for a swim so I went out and got in the water. A few minutes later Joe, Ryan, and Mykel joined us. I looked at the way Ryan kept stealing glances at Mykel and I could tell that she had a thing for him. It's a pity that it will never go anywhere. He looked at Ryan as a lil' sister. She grew up with Bri so he wasn't about to go there with her no matter how bad she wanted it.

They had a beach ball so we played ball in the water. I looked over to where Bri was and she looked comfortable taking a nap on KB's shoulder. If I had my phone by me I'd take a picture. This pregnancy was talking all my sister's energy and she wasn't even past the first trimester yet. I made a mental note to ask when she was going to tell our family.

We stayed on the beach soaking up the sun for a couple hours before we all went in and showered. After that we got in one of the trucks and headed out so that we could find food and drinks.

CHAPTER NINE

KHALIL

Three months have passed since the trip to Jamaica and things were finally back on track between me and Bri. We were back to our date nights and sleeping under the same roof every night. Not to mention our sex life is amazing. Bri's hormones are all over the place so she's always horny. It feels good as hell fucking every day without having to worry about pulling out.

We're back to splitting days between each other's house right now. That's all good right now, but eventually once the baby gets here that's going to have to change. I want to be there every step of the way of my child's life, and bouncing between two houses is not going to work.

If it was up to me, we'd be living under one roof by now, but I know that's not what Bri wants. She already told me she'd never move inside of another man's house again after she almost ended up homeless when her ex died. The only way she'll live with another man is if they went and got a house together, but that doesn't make any sense right now since we both own our places.

By the time the baby gets here I'll more than likely move into her house since she has more space but still keep my condo. She's only five months pregnant right now so we still have a few months to figure everything out.

We're on the way to our gender reveal right now and I'm anxious to see what we're having. We went to the doctor two weeks ago for the ultrasound and the results were sent to Hailey and my mother. They're the only two that know what we're having.

Originally we weren't having one but then Hailey begged us so we agreed. Since it was her idea, the reveal is being thrown at my parents' house. I'm sure my father was the one that paid for everything. He's happy that he's going to be a grandfather so he's not tripping about it.

My family is just as excited about the baby as me and Bri. I already know they're going to be trying to kidnap my baby all the time. I'm cool with that though because that means my kid will be loved and I won't have babysitting issues when I need to spend alone time with my woman.

We pulled up to my parents' house and the sound of music was playing. There was a sign in the front lawn and the smell of barbecue was in the air. I hadn't eaten since breakfast time so I was hungry as hell.

The driveway was full and there were no parking spots in the front of the house so I parked in the garage. I got out of the car and walked over to Bri's side of the car and helped her out.

"You're good baby?" I asked.

"Yeah, just a little tired," she answered.

"We'll only be here for a couple hours then we can go back to my house and I'll tuck you in."

Bri smiled then held my hand as we walked to the backyard where the event was being held. There were pink and blue decorations all over the yard. People were standing around talking and filling out index cards.

"Hey, y'all finally made it," Hailey beamed, hugging us both.

"Hey, sorry we're late. That was my fault. I didn't like how any of my clothes were fitting," Bri admitted.

"Girl, don't be crazy, you're beautiful," Hailey complimented her.

"I told her that but she said I was only saying that because it was my job as her man," I added.

Ever since Bri's last doctor's appointment she was feeling self-conscious about her weight since she gained ten pounds. Her doctor told her that it was normal but that only went in one ear and out the other. It wasn't like she was gaining weight just to be gaining it. She was carrying a child. The weight gain isn't even that noticeable because it's not like she's getting fat. The weight is going to her ass, thighs, and breasts. I like the weight on her and she's carrying it well. She's twenty-one now and growing into her grown woman body.

Hailey guided us over to a table that had team boy or team girl buttons on it. Bri was convinced she was having a girl and I didn't care what we had as long as the baby was healthy so I was following her lead. We both put on team girl buttons then we walked around to greet our guests. It was an intimate occasion so we didn't invite a lot of people. It was just our close family and friends.

My mom and sister did a good job planning this. They were always good at this kind of stuff. Everything was set up like a carnival. There was a snow cone machine, ice cream machine, a popcorn stand with cotton candy, and a candy table. My pops and Joe were on the grill. They had even hired a DJ. If they did all this for a reveal I can only imagine how the baby shower is going to be.

"Hey, you look beautiful Bri," my mother spoke before hugging both of us.

"Hey, thank you Mrs. Beckford," Bri replied.

"Bri, you're having my grandchild so that means you're family now. I told you to call me Hilary or Ma."

"Let her be Ma, she'll do that when she's comfortable," I said, speaking up for her.

"Okay, well Bri why don't you go sit down at our table up front and I'll make you a plate after talking to my son," my mom suggested, making me look at her strange.

"Alright, thank you," Bri replied before walking away.

My mother turned around and started walking toward the house. I followed her until we got to my father's den where no one could hear us. She had me nervous and curious at the same time as she closed the door. I was wondering what she had to talk to me about that needed this much privacy.

"When was the last time you've heard from Krystal?" my mother asked out of nowhere.

"I don't know, like four months ago. Why are you asking me about her?"

"She's been calling me for the past week. I finally answered this morning and she told me that she's pregnant."

"What does that have to do with me?"

"She said it's your baby."

"Well she's lying, I only have one baby on the way."

"Well I think you should give her a call. You did sleep with her so it could be possible."

"Ma, I said it's not my baby. No disrespect, but I'm not about to talk about this right now. I need to get back to Bri before she thinks something is wrong," I told her, walking out.

I headed back outside and found Bri sitting down talking to her sister.

"Is everything okay?" Bri asked, looking up at me.

"Yeah, she just wanted to check and see how things were between us," I lied. There was no use in telling her about the conversation we had because it wasn't true. There's no way Krystal could be pregnant and I didn't know about it. Kenya would have said something or she would have came to the trap and told me. I watched her take the morning after pill so I don't know what's with these crack-head games. I was going to call her later though and get on her ass for involving my mother in this shit. She knows I don't play when it comes to my family and their feelings. Got my mama thinking I'm backing out from my responsibilities.

Everyone sat around talking and playing a couple games before my sister turned on a slide show. It was pictures of me and Bri from some of our date nights and family outings. There were even pictures of each stage and month of the pregnancy. It was thought out and put together nicely. Everyone applauded when it ended and Bri's hormonal ass was sitting over here crying. I pulled her into my arms and kissed her softly on the lips.

"Okay, now the moment we have all been waiting for is finally here. Can the happy couple come up front so that we can see what they're having?" Hailey announced.

The music went silent as we got up to walk toward the front. Blue and pink fireworks were going off as Joe wheeled a table out with a big ass cake on it. Once the fireworks stopped my mom handed Bri a knife. She took her time cutting the cake and when she pulled the slice out it was pink. That meant Bri was right about us having a girl.

"It's a girl," Bri yelled, jumping into my arms causing people to cheer with us. I leaned down, kissing her on the lips. I was so caught up with what was going on around us that I didn't pay attention to my surroundings. I had went against my top rule.

"Congratulations daddy, looks like you're going to have a boy and girl," Krystal shouted from the front of the yard, getting our attention. I knew she was about to cause a scene so I rushed over to her before she could. I grabbed her arm and dragged her inside of the house and to the living room so that no one could hear us.

"What the fuck are you doing here?" I asked through gritted teeth.

"I came to see my baby daddy. It was only right that I showed up at your gender reveal so that you could know the gender of both of your kids."

"Both of what kids? You're not pregnant with my child," I said, looking down at her protruding belly. She wasn't as big as Bri, but she looked like she could be about four months pregnant so there's a chance that this might be my baby.

"What the hell is going on here?" Bri asked from behind me, catching me off guard.

"Are you going to tell her or should I?" Krystal smirked. I wanted to knock that damn smirk off her face.

Bri eyes roamed from me to Krystal then back to me. It was like a lightbulb registered in her head.

"Are you still fucking her and is that your baby?" Bri inquired.

"Hell no, I told you I wouldn't do that again," I replied.

"Girl, he's lying to you. Yes this is his baby and yes we're still fucking," Krystal lied.

I know that one lie was about to ruin my relationship. There was no way I could prove I wasn't sleeping with her and I couldn't prove that she's not carrying my baby.

"That's how you're going to do me Khalil? I forgave you and I've been nothing but faithful, and this is how you replay me?"

"Come on Bri, you can't believe her. She's saying all this to break us up. I haven't talked to her since that night everything happened."

"You think I'm stupid Khalil? She wouldn't be doing all this if it wasn't a possibility that the baby is yours. I'm so over your lying ass and this relationship," Bri yelled, turning away.

"Bri wait," I said, grabbing her by the arm. I don't why I did that because all it did was further piss her off. She started throwing punches my way. I kept grabbing her fists trying to block some of the hits.

"That's enough! Brielle, stop, you have to think about your baby," my mama yelled, causing Bri to step back.

"Baby, calm down, we can talk about this," I pleaded. If I had actually been cheating I wouldn't be tripping, but I'd been faithful to her since she took me back.

"I don't have shit to talk about. You're making me sick just looking at you right now."

"You getting worked up for nothing, I didn't—" I started, but she cut me off.

"I don't wanna hear the lies that come out of your mouth. You can go be with that bitch. I promise me and mine are good over here," she told me before storming through the house.

I was about to run after her my mother stopped me.

"Don't, going after her will make things worse. She's pregnant and doesn't need the stress. You need to sit here and take care of this situation," she said before walking away.

I rubbed my hand over my face, frustrated. I couldn't believe I had finally got my relationship back and just that quick, it was crumbling behind a lying bitch. I couldn't help but look at Krystal. She had come in and started all this shit. She was nothing compared to Brielle. She was fake from the ass to the breasts. I didn't even feel like looking at her to be fucking honest. The longer I looked the more I was ready to smack fire from her ass.

"Are you going to say something or you're just going to keep staring?"

"Bitch, don't get smart with me. Why the fuck did you lie like that, and how many months are you?

"I needed to get your attention, and I'm four months."

"Where's your ultrasound or paperwork?" I asked,

Reaching in her purse, she pulled out an ultrasound and handed it to me. I looked at the date and name on it. She just found out what she was having yesterday. I'm guessing her sister told her about this and she showed up.

"Why did you wait so long to tell me?"

"I knew that if I would have told you when I first found out you would have made me get an abortion."

I couldn't argue with her there because she was definitely right. I feel like she's doing all this shit on purpose because she knows I don't want a baby with her, but at the same time I'll take care of my responsibilities.

"I want a DNA test," I finally said, causing her to give me a hurt look.

"How could you even ask me for a DNA test? You know you the only nigga I been with."

"No I don't know that because you know you fuck around Krystal. Your ass not celibate when we're not together."

"Why you standing here acting like I'm a ho or something? You know that I love you Khalil. Did you ask that bitch for a DNA test? Didn't you end up in my bed because she cheated?"

"Mind your motherfucking business and don't call her no bitch. She didn't cheat on me and if she did, what I do with her doesn't concern you," I reminded her.

"You're right, that's my bad. I just want you to be there for me like you are for her. Our son deserves a family too," Krystal pouted as tears welled in her eyes.

I was weak when it came to women crying, so I pulled

her into my arms to console her. She didn't need to be stressing whether she was carrying my child or not. Once she was calm I took a step back. I didn't want to give her the wrong idea.

"Look, if that baby is mine I'll be there to help take care of both of you financially. In the meantime, I can go to doctors' appointments with you and pick up medication, but that's where it ends at. If it's not about the baby we don't have shit to talk about. I can't treat you like Bri because that's my woman and I plan on getting her back. She's the only woman I'm laying up with and giving this dick to."

"What if she doesn't take you back? Will I have a chance then?" she had the nerve to ask.

I looked at her dumb ass like she was crazy. I know she didn't even think it would be a chance in hell I even let her sniff my dick again after this shit.

"Hell nah, even if you had a chance it's over with now. I can't trust you to keep your mouth closed. You just lied and fucked up what I was building with her for the second time. I couldn't be mad about the first time because you told the truth about what happened between us, but this time you just lied with a straight face and you ruined our event. I know all of this was done with malice intent because if you really wanted to let me know about the baby, you would have reached out to my brother like you do all the other times I block you, and not my mother."

"So how am I going to reach you to discuss stuff about the baby if I'm blocked?"

"I'm going to unblock you, but if it's not an emergency don't call me after 7 or I'm blocking you again and you'll have to go through my family to reach me," I advised her.

I was done with this topic and I really needed to get back to Bri, so I walked Krystal out to her car and of course, Kenya was sitting in the car. She was always twisting the knob in Krystal's back.

"I knew you weren't far behind. You're the one that told her the details about this gender reveal. I'm so glad my brother came to his senses and left your ass alone," I said, walking away without giving her a chance to respond. I walked back to where everybody was and I couldn't find Bri anywhere, so I finally went to ask my mom did she see her.

"If you're looking for Bri she's gone. Joe took her and Stacey home," my mom said before I got the chance to ask.

"Why would he do that without saying anything?" I yelled, getting some people's attention.

"Aye, calm that noise down. It was either Joe take her home or she was about to try and order an Uber. There was no way she was going to stick around here," my pops added.

I was so fucking mad I didn't know what to do so I just went back in the house. I didn't want to be bothered with anybody so I went and sat in my father's den. I tried to call Bri and it went straight to voicemail, so I called Joe's phone instead.

"What's up?" he answered calmly.

"You know what's up? Where y'all at?"

"I'm about fifteen minutes from Bri's house."

"Okay, I'm about to slide that way," I told him.

"Not yet, let me try and calm her down some first. She threatened to leave if you started showing up at the house again."

"Aight, but I'm not waiting two weeks again. She gets two days tops," I said before hanging up.

I sat in my pops' office for I don't know how long until he came in. He poured both of us a glass of cognac then handed me one before sitting down.

"What's going on with you, son? You've been doing a lot of

fucking up lately when it comes to your relationship. I thought you loved Brielle."

"I do, Krystal's ass is lying about us still fucking around. I only slept with her the one time that Bri knew about. I did slip up and nut in her, but I bought the morning-after pill immediately after. I don't think that baby is mine."

"Well, you might not want to hear this, but since there is a possibility, you should leave Bri alone until the DNA test results come back."

"What? Why would I do that?"

"Because what's the point of fighting for a relationship that's only going to come to an end in a few months if those results come back positive? Do you think Bri is going to stick around for that, and do you think Krystal is going to stop interfering with your relationship?"

My father had a good point, but I wasn't willing to go that long without being with Bri. I had damn near went crazy when it was just two weeks and he's talking about five and half months.

"How did you know Ma was the one?" I randomly asked.

"She was the only woman that I dated that I couldn't imagine my life without. She was beautiful, smart, driven, and always had my best interest at heart. Even when I fucked up and things got rocky, she never left my side. She was with me for me and not what I could do for her. I had to snatch her up because I didn't want another man to be with her." He smiled proudly.

"That's the kind of woman I want to settle down with. I see all that in Bri. I know I haven't known her for that long but she makes me feel things I've never felt. She's a different kind of breed. I'm not willing to lose her," I admitted.

"Son, from you sitting here having this conversation with me, that lets me know that she's the one for you. There's no time stamp on falling for someone or loving them. I'm not telling you to run off and get married right now, but you two are having a baby, so even if the relationship doesn't work you need to be there for your daughter. This is a fucked-up situation but you have to go with her flow. Don't pressure her into anything. All you can do is take baby steps, and it's up to her if she wants to work on y'all."

We sat in silence finishing our drinks before switching to business. I allowed what my father told me to sink in, but patience isn't my strong suit. I need to speak with Bri and see what my options are, so she had two days to reach out before I show up at her doorstep.

CHAPTER TEN
BRIELLE

Today I woke up in my feelings and feeling sorry for myself. That's pretty much how it has been the past couple of days since I found out Khalil possibly has another baby on the way. I was feeling hurt and empty inside. I was sitting on my couch eating some Oreo ice cream and listening to hurt hoe music.

"See I done been lied to, backstabbed, and heartbroken. I wanted to cry but I was too afraid to open. Prayin' one day I'd find a peace of mind by the ocean. I spent all my time committing crimes to get closer.

"While at my nana house I play the couch, starin' at the ceiling. Tryin' not to get in my feelings. Thinking' of a way I could make these millions. Maybe that'll take this pain away and clear up all these rainy days, yeah," I sang along with Rod Wave to "Heart on Ice." He was one of the artists I loved to listen to when I was in my feelings.

"Heart been broke so many times I don't know what to believe

Mama say it's my fault, it's my fault, I wear my heart on my sleeve

Think it's best I put my heart on ice, heart on ice 'cause I can't breathe

I'ma put my heart on ice, heart on ice, it's gettin' the best of me," Stacey came in singing along with me.

I felt the tears from my eyes and I hurriedly wiped them away. I was tiring of crying over Khalil. For a minute he had me thinking something was wrong with me. I had to look myself in the mirror and remind myself that even though I'm pregnant, I'm still a bad bitch. I was the catch in our relationship, not the other way around. He really had me fucked up. It took everything in me not to call and curse him out these past two days. The crazy part about it is he hasn't even reached out to me. Joe said he was giving me a couple days, but I didn't believe it at first. I was grateful that he was giving me the time that I needed, so if he called me today I'd answer his call.

"I would ask how you're doing today but judging by the ice cream, I got my answer. I know one thing though, you better snap out of this depressed shit because my niece needs real food," Stacey pointed out, sitting next to me.

"I know, this is my last day. After this I'm going back to being the bad bitch I am," I replied.

"Good, where's your best friend?" Stacey asked, referring to Ryan.

"I'm not sure, she was gone when I got up. She told me she had found a few apartments so she's probably out looking at them," I replied.

After the trip to Jamaica we came back and had the meeting. I thought about it for almost a week before I decided it was best for everyone to move out. I needed to be able to sleep comfortably at home, especially with a baby on the way. I needed Stacey here with me and she wasn't getting along with Jayde, so it was never going to work. I gave them a three-month notice. Jayde and Lena were out within a month. They went and moved in the dorms. Ryan needed a little bit more time because she was going to have to do everything on her own, so I gave her until the baby was born.

At first I was going to let her stay, but then I thought about my baby needed a room and so did Stacey. I wanted my office back because once the baby gets here I'll be finishing school online.

We did say we'll try to rebuild our friendship, but that's going to take time because I don't trust her right now. Right now I'm already dealing with relationship issues and a pregnancy. I don't have the energy to worry about anything else.

It made me sick to my stomach just thinking about the fact that Khalil may have been cheating on me this entire time. How could he put not only me in danger but our baby as well? He knows I don't play when it comes to my health. Just thinking about all of this got me ready to go to his crib and knock him upside his shit.

Everything was finally going good between us. We were finally back on track. Now I was starting to think that our relationship wasn't meant to be. All kinds of shit had been going through my head these last couple of days and none of it was good.

Imagine talking to and seeing someone every day then not seeing them at all. I was going to bed wrapped up in arms and waking up the same way. He was a big part of my life.

I think most of all I miss the sex. He had me coming every single night whether we were making love or he was eating me out. I don't think I ever needed some dick so bad in my life. Hot tears instantly fell from eyes. This pregnancy has my emotions and hormones all over the place.

"Stop crying Bri, it's going to be okay," Stacey said, pulling me into her arms causing me to cry harder.

"No it's not, I miss him so much. I need some dick," I cried.

"Bitch, are you serious? You been sitting here crying over dick when I'm thinking you're depressed?"

"Shit, I am depressed. I went from getting good dick to a drought. Who does he think he is to do this to me?" I asked seriously.

"Girl, for one, it's not a drought because it's only been a couple days. If you want some dick that bad call and tell him to come over. Get your nut off then send him away," I replied.

"I'm not calling him first. However, when he does call I might go with your suggestion," I stated. Hell, why should I have to suffer because of his fuck up?

"Good, now we can get rid of this ice cream and you can go wash your ass," Stacey joked.

"Bitch, don't play with me. I might've been in my feelings but I definitely got in the shower and washed my ass. I just didn't do anything to my hair."

"I know, I'm just kidding. Believe me, if your ass stank for real I would've been came out here and drug you to the shower," she said, causing me to laugh.

We started discussing what we were going to eat when my phone started ringing. I looked down and saw that it was Khalil calling.

"Speak of the devil," I stated before answering the phone.

"I'm going to go upstairs and give you some privacy," Stacey told me, excusing herself. I was glad that she chose to go upstairs because I didn't feel like moving right now.

"What?" I answered, pressing the phone to my ear.

"Damn, that's how we answer for each other now?" he asked, smacking his lips.

"Be glad that I answered," I stated with a slight attitude.

"Yo, chill with that attitude shit. That bitch is lying about me still fucking her. It only happened the one time that you know about."

"Okay, but there is a possibility that the baby is yours right?"

"Yeah, but I think she's lying about that too."

"Well, I guess we won't know until you get a DNA test, which I'm sure you plan on getting."

"Of course I am. Now how you and my baby doing?" he asked, changing the subject.

"We're doing good. I've just been resting," I replied as I rubbed my stomach. I needed to be more conscious of my baby's health. I'm just grateful she's growing strong and healthy after all the stress I've been through.

"That's good. So have you had time to think about us?" he inquired.

"Honestly, right now I just want to focus on our daughter and have a healthy pregnancy. I can't deal with the negative energy and wondering what you're doing behind my back. I need you to be here for our daughter or keep it moving. Once the DNA test is done then we can discuss us."

"I don't like having to wait but I understand. I'll always play my role as the baby's father. I'll call and check on y'all every day and I'll still be at every doctors' appointment. If you call then I'm there."

"Okay, my next appointment is in two weeks. I'll text you the details."

"Alright, I'll be there. What did you eat today?"

"Oreo ice-cream," I mumbled.

"Brielle, I know damn well you fed my baby something more than ice cream," he yelled, making me feel like a child being chastised.

"Don't yell at me, you know I'm sensitive right now," I reminded him.

"I'm sorry, but you know you're supposed to eat better than that. You're eating for two now."

"I know, damn, I already feel bad enough. That was what I had a taste for at the time."

"Well what do you have a taste for now? I can go grab you something and bring it to you or I can have it delivered," he offered,

"What I got a taste for a dasher driver can't give me," I said.

"Shit, I can feed you this dick but first you got to feed my baby some food. So what you want from a restaurant?" he asked, with his cocky ass. He knew that's what I loved most about him.

"You can get Panda Express. I want the walnut shrimp, orange chicken, and chow mein noodles."

"Okay, I gotcha."

"No wait, I think I want the rice and some broccoli too. So you can take the chow mein off."

"Bri, I'm not about to play with you. I'm just going to order the family meal. Joe supposed to be going to see your sister later so between everybody it'll get eaten."

"Alright, thank you," I said before hanging up.

I debated on if I wanted to go change my clothes or not. I was in my depressed mood so I showered and put on one of Khalil's t-shirts and a pair of boy shorts. I didn't want him thinking I was wearing his shirt because I was thinking about him. The truth is ever since I've been pregnant, I hate wearing clothes. If I wasn't down here I wouldn't even have on under-wear. Clothes be having me feeling confined. Stacey and Khalil keep trying to get me to go buy maternity clothes but I'm not ready for that yet. I'm good with my leggings and shirts.

I turned my music back on and laid across the couch. I laid there for about forty-five minutes until the sound of my door-bell went off. I looked at my camera app and saw that it was Khalil. He must've been nearby if he was able to get food and make it here so quick.

I got up from the couch and opened the front door.

"Hey, that was quick," I said.

"Yeah, I was already out when I called you."

"I figured that, thanks for the food."

"Damn, you not letting me stay to eat?"

"What you trying to eat?"

"See, that's why your ass pregnant now. Go feed my niece then y'all can get back to that freaky shit," Stacey stated, walking over to us taking the bags from Khalil.

"What's up Stacey," Khalil spoke.

"Hey KB," she spoke back.

I walked toward the dining room while Khalil closed and locked the door. I sat at the table as Stacey grabbed plates and silverware from the cabinet.

"You want a Sprite or cranberry juice?" Khalil asked, walking over to the refrigerator.

"You can get me a Sprite," I answered.

"Me too," Stacey added.

I grabbed one of the plates and put everything on it. Now that my morning sickness was over I was back to being able to eat everything. I still watched how much I ate though because if I overeat, my baby balls up in a tight knot and my stomach starts cramping.

We sat talking while we ate. Once we were done we went in the front and chilled until Joe showed up. Khalil said he was going to be the only man to see me in boy shorts, and I wasn't about to change so we went upstairs to my room.

As soon as we made it in he locked the door and pulled me toward the bed.

"Now what was that shit you was talking on the phone? You said you wanted to eat this dick?" he questioned, pulling down his pants and boxers.

I opened my mouth to say something and before I could, he was stuffing his length in my mouth trying to make me deep throat him.

"Fuck," he groaned as he hit my tonsils.

"Hmmm," I hummed on his dick.

"Shit, just like that baby," he groaned, pushing my head down further causing me to almost gag.

"Fuck that, let me get some of this pussy." He pulled out of my mouth and lifted my shirt then pulled down my underwear.

He laid down on the bed and I got on top of him, sliding down his dick. Now that I was five months pregnant we weren't comfortable doing missionary anymore and he loved when I rode his dick.

"Oh my god, Khalil," I panted once all of his length was inside of me.

He held onto my waist and lifted me up and down, helping me to adjust to his size. No matter how much we have sex I still have to get adjusted.

"Fuckkkk," he said, trying not to groan too loud.

The sounds of his groans had my head pumped up. I was twerking and twirling on his dick even though he was tearing up my insides.

My walls started to contract, indicating that my orgasm was near.

"Khalil baby, waittt. I'm about to cummmm," I moaned as my sweet juices slid down his dick.

He carefully lifted me off of him and flipped me over,

entering me from the back. He was holding onto my ponytail and waist, giving nothing but back shots. I knew if I wasn't pregnant he'd be tearing my ass up, but he was nervous about hurting me or the baby. Another ten minutes went by before he was busting inside of me.

I allowed him to catch his breath before getting up from the bed and going in the bathroom. I brushed my teeth and got in the shower. Once I was done I wrapped a towel around me and walked back in the room where Khalil was half asleep.

"Khalil, get up so that you can shower. I need to change these sticky sheets."

He got up from the bed and went in the bathroom. I moisturized my body then put on a pair of boy shorts and a tank top. I didn't plan on going back downstairs no time soon. After that I changed my sheets and climbed in bed just as Khalil was coming out the bathroom with nothing but dick swinging. Any other time I would've been ready for a part two, but I got what I wanted and I was satisfied.

Khalil looked in the drawer on his side and took out a fresh pair of boxers and a tank top. Once he was done putting them on he attempted to climb in my bed, but I stopped him.

"'Nah, this ain't that kind of party. I meant what I said on the phone. I want us to focus on our baby right now, so that means no sleepovers or cuddling."

"Brielle, you can't be serious. You just went from sucking my dick and fucking me to kicking me out. How was that beneficial for our child?"

"It's beneficial because if I'm happy then the baby is happy. I was horny and needed some dick."

"Okay, so how does this situation work between us so that I'm clear?"

"You'll feed me if I have cravings. You'll go to all my doctors' appointments with me. You'll give me head if I need my pussy ate and dick if I ask for it. If you can't handle that then number three and four are off the table, but number one and two are mandatory."

"So basically I'm at your beck and call whenever you want sex, but what about me?"

"Being at my beck and call for sex is beneficial to you. We can have sex at least four days out of the week, and if you have the urge and want to give me head in between that time it can be arranged."

"Okay, so basically we're friends with benefits."

"No sir, friends with benefits means we're allowed to do whatever we want with other people. I can't go fuck somebody else because I'm pregnant. Well, I can, but that would be disrespectful, so you can't either. We're still lovers for now but taking time apart until further notice. These are my terms because if I find out that you out here entertaining other bitches, we will be separated indefinitely because that means you're cheating. I'm offering you sex four days a week. We should be good the other three. We can negotiate the days."

Khalil stood there shocked, not believing my words, but I was serious. I believed him when he said he wasn't cheating with her, but I'm not letting him completely off the hook until a DNA test is done. If it's positive we'll just be coparenting our daughter, because I refuse to have to deal with eighteen years of Krystal.

"Okay, so what if I just want to chill with you or take you out?"

"It depends on how I feel that day. Between school and pregnancy you know I be tired."

"Aight Bri, I'll entertain this shit for now. Next thing I know you gone be paying and thanking me for my services," he grumbled.

"Don't be like that. I still love you and the money that you use for my gifts can be used for the baby right now. I know I might be being difficult, but during this pregnancy this is the only kind of relationship I can do right now."

"I understand, I fucked up again so I'm ready to jump through your hoops. I love you too and I guess I'll call you tonight before I go to bed," he told me before leaning over to kiss me.

I kissed him back then he left the room. Now that I had an orgasm I was tired, so I curled up in bed to take a nap.

CHAPTER ELEVEN
KHALIL

For the past three weeks I've been burying myself in work. I was making drops and dropping niggas. I had to let my presence be known on the streets. I was standing outside the trap house watching interactions and seeing how busy the streets were. I needed to know if these niggas were being lazy and not hustling or if the block they were on was slow. If that would've been the case then I would've moved them to another spot.

Some of my men were on their shit but some were just on bullshit. The ones that were on bullshit and costing me money had to go. I aimed to have a strong empire and there's no room for weak links. During my observations I found out that I have a rat in my camp that needs eliminating. He's been working for me and the competition, skimming off my product. I had been waiting for the perfect time and tonight we were going to make our move.

I had other shit to deal with before that though. I just hired a few chicks to work for me so I needed to make sure they knew their roles.

"Kiana, Nique, get naked and go in the first room. Tone will make sure y'all have everything y'all need. If you don't know how to do something or can't find something, ask. I don't need y'all fucking up my shit," I told them. I was using them to help cut and package the crack. I already had one of the best cookers that money could buy.

"Jenn and Dani, y'all can follow me this way," I said, leading them to the room where money is counted. "The same rules apply to y'all as the other girls. If y'all got any questions, ask somebody. There's men all over in every room that can help."

Once I finished helping them get settled in I went into the drug room where the crack was already packaged and needed to be distributed. I sat down and started counting bricks. Usually my brother would be helping with some of this or some of the other guys, but I needed them on watch for the trap house. I was cool with getting back to the basics. I was using this time to focus on work and not how fucked up my situation is.

I had a lot on my plate, and two women pregnant at the same time was not a good look. The thought of Krystal walking around carrying my baby still had me pissed. The crazy part about this is she's not the one giving me a hard time. She respected what I told her and she doesn't call me at night. I was supposed to go to her doctor's appointment with her last week but she had to reschedule last minute.

I've went to Bri's appointment with her and she barely talked to me. I'm starting to think everything is getting to her now. The fact that I might be having another baby. I guess this is her way of detaching herself from me. We also weren't sleeping together four days out of the week like she offered. I've only slept with her twice since that day. I think she's doing all of this to test if she can trust me or not.

I went from getting my dick wet every day to being in the Sahara Desert. All of this shit was crazy to me. Not to mention her attitude has been fucked up lately. Her ass needs some dick to make her act right. I know she be wanting it but she's being stubborn.

By the time I was finished counting the bricks Joe came walking in. He flopped down in one of the chairs across from me.

"Is everything a go?" I asked Joe as he walked over to me. This should be a quick in and out job so it was only four of us going.

"Yeah, Max and Adam are already there scoping everything out. They just waiting on us so that we can air that bitch out. We split whatever money we find and the drugs go back to inventory."

"Cool, let's go," I said, getting up from the chair. I grabbed my black ski mask and gloves then we left the warehouse and climbed in a black Nissan. It was one of the cars we drove when we had to do a job. The tags were already changed and the car was cleaned after every use.

We drove for almost forty minutes until we made it to Forest Park, Georgia. I signaled for Adam to pull up in the driveway and kill the lights. Joe parked across the street and did the same.

Me and Joe checked our Glocks then put on our ski masks before getting out of the car. We looked around before running across the street.

"Aye Adam, go around back. Max, stay right here out front on look out. Me and Joe going to go through the front door." I made sure everyone followed my orders before kicking in the front door. It made a loud BOOM sound then gunshots started ringing out of nowhere.

I shot back as I went to find Ray's office. Once I found it I signaled for Joe and Adam to get him. They hurriedly grabbed him and led him to the van where Max was to tie him up.

Joe came back in and helped me start knocking shit over and looking for his stash. We had to make it look like a robbery gone wrong.

"Yo, we gotta go, I hear 12," Max yelled in the house.

We grabbed the four duffel bags that we found and ran out of the house. I didn't get a chance to open them and see what was inside but they were bulky. I allowed Adam and Max to pull out and go in one direction while we went the other way. We got away just in time as the police were driving up the block. Instead of speeding I drove at a normal pace so I didn't catch their attention. Once they were out of sight I floored it all the way back to the trap.

By the time we made it Adam and Max had already put Ray in the basement tied up.

"So, you and Mike thought it was cool to steal from me? You didn't think I'd find out?"

"Fuck you nigga, we saw an opportunity and took it," he spat.

"Coo, I'll let those be your final words," I told him before letting off three rounds. BANG, BANG, BANG. Two to the chest and one to the head.

I walked out, leaving the cleanup crew to handle it from here. I wanted to go through the duffel bags and see what was all in them. When I made it upstairs I looked around for Joe and found him in one of the rooms already pulling stuff from one of the bags.

I walked in and sat down next to him and started helping him. An hour later we were done counting and splitting everything. It was three hundred four thousand dollars in cash and ten kilos of uncooked dope. I didn't know exactly how much they had stolen from me but I know I got more in return. I was going to put my cut in Bri's bank account so that she would be good. I didn't want her trying to find a job after having the baby. I wanted her to chill for at least a year.

After a job well done and a good day of work, we decided to go to the lounge we had in the warehouse and chill. We turned on the music then lit a few blunts and poured some drinks. Once the other workers finished their tasks they came and joined us.

I'd been sitting there for almost an hour feeling chill as hell. I was relaxed for the first time in the past few weeks. I was having a good time with my people. My eyes was getting heavy until I felt somebody touch my leg, causing me to snap my head up seeing Nique grinding on my lap, and I didn't mind. She was a dark-skin thick beauty with plump lips. I reached out and started rubbing on her big ass and pussy. I knew that shit was juicy from when I saw her walking around naked earlier.

"You trying to go somewhere more private?" she whispered in my ear, grinding even harder. I licked my lips thinking about it for a minute. I was in need of some pussy or at least head. My nut is built up and Bri is playing. She's not sticking to her end of the bargain, so should I really be depriving myself when this beautiful woman is literally throwing pussy my way?

"Yeah, let's go," I told her, lifting her off my lap. I grabbed her hand and led her down the hall to my room. We got in and closed the door. She immediately unbuckled my pants, causing my phone to fall out of my pocket.

"Hand me my phone," I told her as she dropped to her knees in front of me. I unlocked it, looking at my notifications.

2 Missed Calls: Wifey

Me: Baby, my bad for not picking up. I was taking care of business. Is everything good?

Two minutes passed and she didn't text back, so I sent another text.

Me: Why you not texting back? You mad at me?"

Wifey: Why you just texting me back? I called you almost two hours ago.

Me: I'm sorry, I was busy. What you need?

Instead of texting back she called me. I was about to answer until I felt teeth grazing my dick. Just that quick I forgot I was even getting head, so that says a lot. I wasn't enjoying this shit at all.

"Aye ma, try less teeth," I told her as she continued bobbing her head up and down. I don't know if it was me because I was focused on the conversation with Bri, but her mouth was dry as hell. It felt like sandpaper was rubbing up against my dick.

Another five minutes went by and we weren't getting anywhere.

"Stop Nique, I smoked and drunk to much so ain't no telling when I'm gone nut," I lied, trying not to hurt her feelings. Me not nutting didn't have shit to do with me being intoxicated, but more so with her not knowing what she was doing.

"Maybe you could cum if we fucked," she suggested.

She had me wondering if her pussy was as dry as her mouth before I stick my dick in her. I was willing to try though, so I grabbed a condom from the drawer. I was about to put it on when my phone started ringing again. I couldn't keep ignoring Bri's calls.

I held my finger up to my lip, telling Nique not to say anything before I picked up.

"What's up baby?" I asked.

"What you doing that you can't answer your phone? You

was able to text but not pick up the phone? You with a bitch or something?"

"Come on Brielle, what's wrong ma? You got my location on your phone so you know where I'm at."

"That don't mean shit. Bitches got cars so they can come to you."

I sighed and walked in the bathroom, closing the door behind me. Grabbing the towel from the rack, I used soap and water to scrub my dick. There was no telling where this conversation was going or how long it was going to last. I wasn't in the mood to fuck anymore.

When I walked back in the room, Nique was laying on the bed naked. I was confused because I thought she would have got the hint.

"Hold on one minute Bri," I said, muting the phone real quick then giving Nique my attention. "Get dressed, we gone have to take a rain check," I said.

Nique got out of the bed with a slight attitude, but I didn't care. I was already dealing with Bri's mood swings so that was enough. She never acted like this before. The baby done changed her entire personality right now.

Once Nique was dressed, I followed her out of the room and locked the door before getting back to my call.

"My bad for putting you on hold like that," I said.

"I see you got me fucked up, Khalil. Why did you mute me? Because I know nobody should be calling you this time of night unless it's an emergency."

"I was talking to one of the guys about something. You know I'm still at the warehouse," I replied, getting irritated. I wasn't used to people questioning me and me actually giving answers.

"Yeah okay," she responded like she didn't believe me.

I sat down on one of the couches so I could finish my conversation before rejoining everybody.

"Did you call me just to curse me out?" I asked, changing the subject.

"No, I called because I missed you, but then I got mad because you didn't answer."

"I miss you too, baby. My phone was on silent so I didn't see your calls. I can come over later on today with food," I offered.

"I don't want to wait until later. I'm horny right now," she whispered.

I shook my head because this damn girl was something else. She ain't gave me none in a week and now that she was horny she can't wait a few more hours.

"Let me hear it then."

"Nah, you better come here and hear it before I go back to sleep."

"Bri, it's one in the morning. I'm not trying to come over there this late and then have to go right back out in the middle of night."

I wanted to spend time with her but I didn't want to go this late just to fuck. I wanted to be able to spend the night with her.

"Oh, so you're telling me no? Bet."

"That's not what I was saying."

I was expecting Bri to respond but when she didn't say anything, I took my phone off my ear and realized she hung up on me. She was about to make me snatch her ass up.

I tried calling back and she didn't answer.

"You good bro? Ole girl came back in with an attitude," Joe said, walking over to me.

"Fuck that girl, your sister gone make me ring her neck."

"Who, Brielle?"

"Yeah, this pregnancy got her tripping."

"She probably sexually frustrated."

"Shit, that's not my fault. I'm not holding dick back from her mean ass."

"What happened though? You was just on the phone with her?"

"Yeah, she asked me to come over and I told her I will later."

"Man, you better go see that damn girl before she be ignoring your ass later."

I knew Joe was right. She'd fuck around and block my ass with the quickness. I dapped him up then left the warehouse and headed to Bri's crib. I parked in her driveway then put in the code to open her front door.

I headed up the stairs quietly then turned her doorknob and entered her room. She was lying in bed on her side crying. I sighed before undressing and climbing in bed behind her.

"Talk to me, why you crying?"

She remained silent for a minute before speaking.

"You don't love me no more," she sobbed.

"What? Why would you say some shit like that? I'll always love you no matter what."

"Then why don't you want to make love to me?"

"I never said that Bri. You hung up before I could explain myself. I didn't want to come over just to fuck you then leave out in the middle of the night. I wanted to be able to spend time with you," I explained.

Bri and I laid there talking until she fell asleep, without us having sex. I was starting to think we needed to go to counseling because we're using sex to mask our problems, and that's not healthy for none of us. I want my baby to live in a stable home with her parents. Not us being dysfunctional around her. I'm going to talk to Bri about it when we get up and see if that's something she wants. I think she would and it could be a way for her to build her trust for me again. That could be why she's acting like this. She doesn't trust me and from what happened today, she has every right not to even though I didn't go all the way through with it.

I was getting tired myself so I kissed Brielle on the forehead then held her tight. I rubbed her stomach, causing my baby to kick before I finally fell asleep.

CHAPTER TWELVE
JOE

The bright sun shining through my window woke me out of my sleep. I felt like shit from all the drinking and smoking last night. I leaned over and saw that Nique was still knocked out sleep. After KB left the warehouse she stayed behind smoking and drinking with us. One thing led to another and she was on her way home with me.

I climbed out of bed and went inside the bathroom to take care of my personal hygiene. Twenty minutes later I came out of the bathroom with a towel wrapped around my waist. Nique was still sleep but it was time for her to go. I shook her leg to wake her ass up. It's almost eleven so like a hotel, it's checkout time.

"What time is it? Why are you waking me up?" Nique asked, laying her head back down on the pillow.

"My baby mama on her way with my daughter and I don't feel like dealing with no bullshit."

"Can I at least take a shower first?"

"Make it quick," I told her, looking down at my phone. I wanted her out of here before Kenya came over. I don't deal with Kenya like that anymore but I don't want the shit to get back to Stacey. We're not in a relationship but it's the principle of things.

I got up from the bed and got dressed in a pair of black jeans and a red t-shirt. I looked back down at my phone and saw that Nique had been in the bathroom for almost twenty minutes. I was about to go knock on the door when she came walking out. She didn't bother wrapping a towel around her body. I glanced up at her then went back to checking my messages.

"Yo, what the fuck are you doing?" I asked, getting up and snatching her phone from her. She was taking pictures of me and tagging them on Facebook. I don't know how the hell she found my shit because it's private.

"I sucked your dick last night so I should be able to post you."

I looked at her dumb ass like she had grown an extra head.

"Bitch, are you serious? Just because you sucked my dick doesn't mean I was going to showcase you to the world."

"I thought this was the beginning of something special," she had the nerve to say.

"What the fuck? You joking, right? You was just about to let my brother fuck last night before you came home with me. Ain't shit special about that," I pointed out.

Bitches be wilding and I know this shit gone most likely get back to Stacey. I can't wait to tell KB about this. With the trouble he's having, he'll be glad he didn't fuck her.

"It sounds like you trying to call me a hoe," she said, sounding offended.

"What's your CashApp so that I can send you money to catch an Uber?" I inquired, ignoring her last comment. I wasn't about to go back and forth with her about her hoetivities.

She gave me her CashTag and I sent her one hundred

dollars to thank her for her services. She didn't complain about me paying her so that proved my point.

Her Uber was going to take ten minutes and Kenya was ten minutes away. I could either make her wait in front of the house next door or chance her and Krystal running into each other.

We sat in awkward silence for eight minutes before we went outside to wait for the Uber. It pulled up the same time that Kenya did. Nique had the nerve to lean in and try to hug me, but I took a step back.

"I'll see you later at work," I told her.

"Who was that? You cheating on your new bitch already?"

"Mind your business and watch your mouth in front of my daughter."

"Whatever, don't have her around none of your bitches," she said, mouthing the word bitches. I ignored her ass because I was going to see Stacey and then I was going to my parents' house so that they could see Kylie.

Kenya walked to her car and I walked in the house. I needed to grab my wallet, keys, and jacket. Since Kylie was with me I grabbed her some snacks and her iPad then we went out to my car. I didn't want her complaining about the hour drive so that should keep her occupied.

As I was pulling up to Bri's house Stacey was texting me about Nique. Since I was already here I didn't text back. I helped my daughter out of the car then I rang the doorbell.

A couple minutes went by before KB opened the door.

"Uncle KB," my daughter beamed, running into his arms.

"Hey Ky, you're getting so big."

"Where Stacey?" I asked, walking in the house.

"In the kitchen talking shit to Bri about you."

I shook my head as I walked in the kitchen.

"What the hell are you doing here? You didn't get my text?" Stacey inquired.

"Hey Bri, how are you and my niece doing?" I asked, purposely ignoring Stacey.

"Hey Joe, we're good. I'm going to give you two some privacy," Bri said, grabbing her bowl of fruit and leaving the kitchen.

"So you out here fucking other bitches now?"

"I didn't fuck her. She only gave me head," I admitted.

"Oh, so if I let another nigga eat my pussy you cool with that?"

"Shit, I don't give a fuck," I lied.

"Bet, I want you to remember that," she told me, storming out of the kitchen. I followed her all the way up to her bedroom. I was trying to figure out what was going on with her. Did she want some dick or something?

Stacey sat on her bed, grabbing her phone ignoring me like I wasn't standing here. She started smiling a little too hard for me, so I snatched that bitch from her hand.

"Give me my phone," she said, jumping up from the bed. I turned around and held it a little higher so she couldn't reach. I looked through her call logs and messages and saw Bri was the last person she texted. They both was on some good bullshit right now. Once I was satisfied I handed her phone back to her.

"Are you going to tell me what's going on? You finally ready to admit your feelings for me? I don't get why you're upset and we're not together. I asked you to have a relationship with me and you said no."

Stacey looked at me for a minute before walking over to her dresser. She pulled a piece of paper out and handed it to me. I looked at the paper and realized it was an ultrasound and it had her name on it.

"You're pregnant? How far along?"

"Yes, I'm eight weeks and before you ask, it's yours. I haven't been with any other man since I moved out this way with Bri. I can get a DNA test done if you want."

"You don't have to do that," I said, looking down at the ultrasound. I knew Stacey wasn't out here fucking around. That was why I wanted to be with her.

"Look, I'm sorry about you finding out what happened. I want you to give us a shot. If it doesn't work we can at least say we tried."

"Okay, but I don't do that cheating shit and you need to cut all your hoes off."

"Say less," I told her before kissing her on the lips. I was happy that I was about to have another child. I wanted one so bad that I was tempted to get Kenya pregnant again. Thank God I didn't go through with that plan. I was looking forward to seeing how things were going to turning out between me and Stacey.

We sat upstairs discussing our expectations for our relationship as well as a future for our child. I can't wait to get to the house to tell my mama. She gone freak out knowing that she's about to have two new grandkids instead of one.

Once me and Stacey finished our conversation I decided to leave and go to my mother's house, then I'd come back over. Kylie was spending the night with me so it wasn't like I needed to rush back home.

It took twenty minutes before I was pulling up to my parents' home. I got out of the car with Kylie and put in the code to enter the house. I walked in and saw my mama, father, and sister sitting in the living room. Kylie ran over and hugged them before going in the back to her playroom.

"You're early, where's your brother?"

"He's at the house with Bri right now. I'm not sure if he's coming."

"Why, is everything okay?"

"I know they had an argument yesterday so I guess he's trying to work on his relationship right now."

"I'm going to need the two of you to get it together. Y'all giving me gray hair," my mother exaggerated.

"I know Ma, we're trying. I have an announcement to make."

"What is it?" my father asked.

"Me and Stacey are officially together and she's pregnant."

"Yay, another baby," my sister beamed.

"How the hell we go from one grandchild to a possible four? Y'all forgot how to strap up?" my dad asked.

"Oh leave him alone. Let them have all the babies right now while we're in good health to watch them," my mom said.

"Well you better not get no ideas, young lady," he told Hailey.

"Ugh Dad, you don't to worry about that," she replied.

Me and Pops chilled and watched the game until my mama was done cooking. She made fried chicken, baked macaroni, green beans, and corn bread. She cooked like she was feeding an army. There was so much food left over that she packed up some for Bri, KB, and Stacey. They were glad to hear that because they were trying to figure out what they were going to eat for dinner.

I stayed at my parents' house for an extra hour before I went back to Bri's house to chill with Stacey for the night. We sat and watched a movie with Kylie before we went to bed. I was surprised that Khalil was still there and Bri was allowing him to spend another night. I'm guessing things are going better for them than expected.

CHAPTER THIRTEEN
KHALIL

Over the past couple of months things were getting back on track between me and Bri. We started going to counseling and the therapist asked her if she thought she would ever be able to forgive me. If she couldn't forgive me then we were both wasting our time. Bri told her that she could but she didn't know how to deal with another baby.

I reassured her that even if that baby is mine it doesn't change anything for us. I was convinced that it wasn't my kid now more than ever because it's been three months since Krystal told me about the baby and she hasn't allowed me to go to any appointments. That got me thinking she's talking to another nigga instead. I ain't tripping about it because it's giving me more time with Bri. She makes sure I'm there with her every step of the pregnancy.

All I've been doing lately is taking care of business and working on my relationship. So when the guys suggested we go out, I thought why not. I might as well have a little fun before my baby gets here. Once she's here I'm not going to be going out like that unless Bri is with me. I tried to get her to come tonight but she said it was ghetto to be in the club eight months pregnant. Plus there was a lot of smoke in the air that isn't good for the baby. She had Stacey to keep her comfortable so she wasn't tripping about me going out.

I stood in the VIP section overlooking the crowd. I had my blunt in one hand and a bottle of Henny in another. This was a pure boost for me. The DJ kept talking over the music and announced that we were in the building. That was all it took for people to rush toward our section. I wasn't on that tonight so I allowed three strippers to come in. That was more than enough since it was only me and five of the guys.

She bendin' over but I want some head first, I'on even wanna know what the pussy like
Trippin' too close to fallin' so I'm ballin'
It's crazy my opp got shot but I ain't call it (Sike, slow up)
I come around, niggas gon' put they hoe up
These bitches stay on my channel (Yeah)
Must've seen me on TV (Yeah)
It took me six hours to count a mil' exactly
I'm accurate with the cheese, yeah (Big Bagg)

People danced and rapped along to Money Bagg Yo's "Said Sum."

I smirked as I sat down in my seat watching the dancers. I'm used to this lifestyle but I'll never get used to the attention. Too much attention causes unwelcome problems. I need to always know what's going on around me and I can't do that in a crowd. I appreciated the love but some days I could do without it, and today was one of them. I just wanted a smooth, chill night.

I grabbed one of the stacks of money and started throwing

dollars at the ladies, careful not to touch anyone. These days you never know who's watching you. One of the dancers tried to sit on my lap but I stopped her. There was no way I was going home smelling like a bitch. I was back to getting pussy on the regular and I didn't want to fuck that up for a dance.

"Damn, you turning down a lap dance? That bitch really got you going crazy," Max laughed, but I ain't find shit funny.

"Yo, watch that bitch word before I knock you in yo' shit. Don't ever disrespect my girl like that," I warned him.

"So y'all back together now?" Adam asked.

"That's wifey, she always has been and she always will be," I told him seriously. I was man enough to let it be known I loved my girl. I always thought when niggas downplayed their relationship they were on some gay shit.

"That nigga drunk, just let it go. Don't let it fuck up your night," Joe cut in. I couldn't understand why they was fucking with me when Joe was just sitting back chilling as well. His ass didn't even throw any money their way.

I decided to zone out from them niggas and get back to enjoying my drink and blunt. I was bobbing my head and rapping to the music. I was back having a good time when one of the strippers approached me. Looking up, I saw that it was this stripper Delicious that I used to fuck with a couple years ago.

"Hey KB, you having fun?" she asked in a soft voice.

"Yeah, I'm just chilling. How you been?"

"I'm good, do you want a private dance?" she asked, which was keyword for if I wanted to fuck.

"Nah, not tonight."

"Whattt, you turning down a private session with me? I thought I was your favorite stripper," she pouted.

"You is, but I ain't on that tonight. You can dance for me though and I'll throw some money your way," I offered.

Delicious smiled at that suggestion. Instead of dancing in what she had on, which was only a see-through leotard, she took everything off. She was but ass naked twerking and shaking her ass. My eyes watched as it jiggled.

This other stripper named Cinnamon followed suit and took off all of her clothes as well. She and Delicious started dancing on each other, then next thing you know, they started kissing. My eyes were locked in the entire time and so were the guys.

Delicious laid down on the empty half of the couch across from me and opened her legs wide. She stared into my eyes as she played in her pussy. She was daring me to just sit here and not do nothing.

Had this been a year ago I would have her and her friend in a private room right now sucking on my balls and dick.

Delicious knew how to suck and fuck good, but her pussy ain't have shit on Bri. I wasn't about to risk fucking her then have to avoid having sex with my girl. I can't chance her catching anything while carrying my baby, and I knew for a fact Delicious got around.

Cinnamon collected some money from Keith then walked over where Delicious was laying. She spit in her pussy then started eating her out. I had been to strip clubs before and seen some freaky shit, but never this freaky. Since Cinnamon's ass was tooted up in the air, Max decided to play in her pussy. He was fingering her shit and she was allowing it. Adam felt the need to join in and started sucking on Delicious's breast. This was turning into more than I bargained for. All I knew was these niggas better not pull out they dick or I'm shooting they ass.

They was on some *Players Club* type of freaky shit. I get that we were in a private section and there were only a few of us, but damn. They were taking it too far. The icing on the cake was when Max pulled his fingers out of Cinnamon and licked them. I damn near threw up in my mouth because there was no telling how many niggas' dicks had been inside of her tonight alone.

"Yo, y'all niggas wild as fuck," Keith laughed, shaking his head.

"Nah, more like nasty as fuck," Joe added.

The alcohol was starting to catch up with me and I needed to take a piss, so I left the section and went out to go to the bathroom. As I was leaving the bathroom two girls sitting at the bar caught my attention. I had to do a double take to make sure my eyes weren't playing tricks on me. I sent Joe a text as I headed down the stairs to where the two females was sitting.

"What the hell are you doing at a bar drinking while pregnant?" I yelled, causing Krystal to turn around and damn near jump out her skin.

My eyes roamed her body and stopped at what was supposed be a seven-month baby bump, but instead it was flat as hell. This shit was all starting to make sense. This was why she never wanted me to go to any appointments with her. She played me this entire time. If this was a cartoon, smoke would be coming from my ears right now.

I snatched Krystal off that bar stool by her hair so fast she almost caught whiplash. I dragged her through the crowd by her hair, not caring that people were staring. Kenya was yelling for me to let her sister go, but if she knew what was good for her she'd mind her business and stay in her place.

When we made it outside, I pushed her ass against the wall and examined her. I had to make sure I wasn't tripping because I knew she didn't fuck up my relationship for no shit. Not to mention putting Bri under unnecessary stress.

"Where the fuck is the baby, Krystal?" I asked, already knowing the answer.

"Uhm, I had a miscarriage," she lied.

"Bitch, now is not the time to play with me," I warned her, grabbing her throat.

"KB, let my sister go before I call the police on your ass," Kenya threatened, grabbing my arm.

"Bitch, mind your business," I warned her, snatching my arm away.

"Bro, calm down and let her go before somebody calls the police," Joe said.

I took a deep breath, releasing my grip and allowing Krystal to catch her breath. She bent over panting like a tired dog.

"Bitch, you caught your breath, now speak the fuck up. What happened to the baby?" I asked again.

"There is no baby. I ordered the belly and ultrasound offline."

"Why? Like what the fuck did you plan on accomplishing?"

"I was hoping since you thought I was pregnant you would have sex with me raw and eventually I'd get pregnant for real, but even with everything I did your nose was up that young bitch's ass."

I looked at her, confused by her flawed plan. This bitch was either dumb for real or thought I was, because how was she gone hide a fake belly during sex? And being four months pregnant and just getting pregnant is a big ass difference when it comes to a stomach.

"Yo, I'm not even about to entertain this shit. Stay the fuck away from me. If you see me on the street, cross or go the other way. Don't acknowledge me or shit. I'm about to act like you never existed."

"After everything we've been through over the years, it's come to this? I love you KB, and I know we can work through this," she cried.

"I don't love you. You're a psychotic bitch. If you was on fire I wouldn't piss on you to put you out," I yelled. That was probably a bit harsh, but I didn't give a fuck about her feelings. She didn't care about mine or Bri's. This was a dog-eat-dog world. I was done sparing bitches' feelings.

"You really fell in love with that girl after everything I've done for you. What does she have that I don't?"

"I'm not having this conversation with you again. Have a nice fucking life," I told her, walking away.

"You know what, fuck you Khalil. Fuck you, that bitch, and that baby. I hope they eat shit and die," she shouted behind my back.

I stopped dead in my tracks after hearing those words. I turned around, and the look on her face was priceless. There was nothing but regret in her eyes because she knew she had just fucked up.

She turned around on her heels and started running, and I was right behind her. She didn't get too far because of her shoes. She lost her balance and landed on her ass. She ain't have on no panties so her pussy was out on display.

"Let me tell you one motherfucking thing. You better be lucky your dumb ass fell because I was about to slap fire from your ass. If you ever think to do something to my woman or child, I will kill your ass without hesitation. You know not to fuck with me like that," I told her before walking away while Kenya helped her up.

Joe and I rode together, and he knew after that I was ready to go. We left without even telling the guys bye. I was pissed and relieved all at the same time. This shit was finally over with and now Bri could give me her all again.

When we made it back to Bri's house it was late, but I couldn't wait to tell her what happened. I stripped out of my clothes then shook her lightly.

"Khalil, I'm tried, that's why I gave you some before you left," she mumbled.

"That's not why I'm waking you up, but while we on the subject, another round won't hurt."

"What's so important?" she asked, turning around on her other side to face me.

"Okay, I'll give you the cliff notes version right now. I ran into Krystal at the club and the bitch not pregnant. She made it all up in hopes to break us up and that I would choose her."

"Are you fucking serious? If I wasn't pregnant, I'd beat her ass. I know she better stay away from us," Bri said.

"You don't have to worry about that. I checked her for the dumb shit she pulled.

"Well, look on the bright side of things. We don't have the doom and gloom of a paternity test hanging over our heads."

"That is so true. Now about that second round." I smirked.

"Fine, but you're doing all the work," she mumbled, turning back over and shifting her ass toward my dick.

This was the main benefit of sleeping naked and having a woman that slept the same way. It was easy access every time.

CHAPTER FOURTEEN
BRIELLE

Once again everything was back to normal between me and Khalil. I was actually nervous to say the least, because as you can see, that's when shit hits the fan. I've been stress free, which is a good thing for me and baby. I only have about a month left before I'll meet my beautiful daughter. After careful consideration, Khalil is going to move in with me temporarily, and then once Stacey has her baby Joe is going to move in with her at my house and then I'll move in with Khalil.

I refuse to sell my house because of the track record we have. I told him if everything is good between us by time the baby is one year old, then we can start looking for houses together.

I was currently standing in my closet trying to figure out what I was going to wear. Khalil has some business to handle so me, Stacey, Ryan, and one of my classmates, Angie, are going out to eat. I was excited about that because if I'm not going to class or on a date with Khalil I don't go out much because my feet be swole.

"I like the black dress," Khalil said from behind me, poking me in the ass with his manhood.

I turned around to look at him, examining his naked body. His dick was standing at attention as always.

"I thought you had to get to work," I said.

"I do, but it's going to be a late night so we need to take care of this problem first," he replied, looking down at his dick.

"Okay, but we only have thirty minutes," I told him, knowing damn well if he needed more time I wasn't going to stop him.

I pushed him back on the bed and our lips connected for what seemed like forever. I can sit and kiss this man until my lips go numb. His dick was jumping against my pussy, begging to make its way into my honey pot.

I kept my hand on the back of his neck to deepen our kiss. We were tongue tied, and I didn't wanna stop. It was something about kissing that was so intimate to me. With the right person it contained more passion than sex.

He rolled me off of him and I got on all fours, arching my back. His index finger glided along my smooth love box. His thick tongue licked all of my juices. He was humming against me, only making me wetter. The only sounds in the room were my loud moans and his slurping. He was licking me like a dehydrated dog outside in one hundred degree weather.

He spread my cheeks apart as he continued to slobber all over my pussy. His fingers pumping in and out of me made me grab onto his sheets.

"Fuck," I dragged out, feeling my stomach tighten. He didn't stop eating, instead he picked up the pace. He had my ass running and gripping the sheets.

"Bri, stop running before you fall on your stomach and hurt my baby," he said before going back to flicking his tongue rapidly like he never stoppered.

My body was shaking and I felt a wave of energy leave from my body as I squirted all over his face. He made sure to lick every drop before positioning his thick dick at my opening.

He rubbed himself against me before he entered. He grunted as he slowly pumped himself inside of me. My insides were going crazy and my baby was doing back flips in my stomach. It was always a weird combination now that the baby was bigger.

He took his time sliding in and out of me. It was a mixture of pain and pleasure.

His pelvis slapping against my ass made me scream out.

"Ugh, fuck baby," I cried out as I came again.

What was supposed to be a thirty-minute session turned into two rounds of mind-blowing sex. After that I didn't have the energy to move. All I wanted to do was cuddle and make love to my man all night.

"Do you have to go?" I whined as we went in the bathroom to take another shower.

"Yes I do ma, I need to get as much work done as I can before the baby gets here because I'm taking off time to be with y'all. Plus you already planned a night with the girls. You deserve a night out. I'll tell you what though. When I get in tonight I'll wake you up to some bomb ass head," he told me, causing me to smile. That was always the best way to wake up.

We finished our shower then he got dressed in a pair of black jogging pants, a black t-shirt, and a black hoodie. From the way he was dressed I knew that meant he was going to handle business in the streets and not in the warehouse. We never discussed his work. He made sure to keep the street shit out in the streets. I don't ask questions and he doesn't volunteer answers. It's the best way to keep me safe. The less I know the better.

I got dressed in a black bodycon dress and a pair of sandals. I combed my curls out and applied a light coat of makeup.

"Shit, you got me ready to stay at home now. You looking good as fuck. I'm going to have to hurry up and put a ring on your finger so these niggas will know you off limits," Khalil complimented me.

"Thanks baby, please be safe out there and come back home to me."

"Always, if you need me I'm only a call away. Y'all be safe and let me know when you make it home. I love you."

"I love you too," I replied before leaning in to kiss him. We always kissed when one of us was leaving and when we got back.

I grabbed my purse and keys then headed downstairs where Stacey was sitting waiting for me. She looked cute in her white dress with her baby bump. I couldn't believe we were having kids a few months apart. Our kids were going to have a chance to grow up with each other. That was something we both wished we had.

Stacey and I left the house and headed to Busy Bee Cafe Soul Food restaurant. I had been having a fast for this all week so I couldn't wait to eat.

"Hello ladies, it'll just be you two?" the tall, slim hostess asked.

"No, we have two more joining us," I answered."

"Alright, right this way. Would you like a table or booth?" she asked.

"A table, this belly ain't making it in no booth," I laughed.

"How far along are you two?" she inquired, leading us to our table.

"I have a few weeks to go," I replied.

"I'm a little over four months," Stacey added.

"Well congratulations. Can I start you off with something to drink?"

"You can get four waters and four Sprites," I ordered for all us. By the time the waiter came back with our drinks Ryan and Angie walked over to the table. We greeted them and then they sat down across from us.

Me and Ryan's relationship was back to a good space. I don't know if I'll call her best friend right now but she's back to a friendship level. We don't hang out much but we do talk on the phone all the time. She offered to help out with the baby when she gets here, but I don't know about that.

Angie is one of the closest friends I have from school. She's smart as hell like me so we have a lot of classes together. We sat around talking one day and we connected. Typically we'd have lunch at school together, but since I switched to online now we started meeting up more.

We picked up our menus and started looking over it. We wanted to be ready to order when the hostess comes back with our drinks.

"Hello ladies, my name is Claire and I'll be your waiter. Are you ready to order?" a short, light-skinned waiter asked.

"Yes, we're ready," I said.

"Ok, what can I get you?"

"I'll have the turkey, dressing, cabbage, and cornbread," said Angie.

"I'll have the smothered pork chops, rice with gravy, black eyed peas, and cornbread," Ryan ordered.

"I'll have the fried catfish, three wings fried, mac and cheese, greens, and cornbread," I stated proudly, not caring that it seemed like a lot of food. What I don't eat now I'll eat later.

"I'll have the catfish, one smothered pork chop, rice, and black eyed peas," Stacey ordered as her eyes scanned the menu.

"Alright, coming right up," the waitress announced before walking away.

"See, that's why you can't go eating with pregnant women. Y'all be ordering the whole menu," Ryan joked.

"Girl, shut up, I'm not about to eat all of this right now. I didn't know how to pick. I was tempted to order a pork chop too but I thought that would be pushing it. Whatever I don't eat will go to Khalil."

"Her fat ass lying. What she don't finish here she'll finish in the car," Stacey countered.

"Bitch, you're one to talk with that weird ass combination of food," I replied.

"So what, I ain't flexing like I'm not going to eat it." She shrugged.

We sat around and talked about what was going on in our lives. I discussed how I felt about becoming a new mom. I was excited that my daughter was finally going to be here. I wondered if she'd have my complexion and Khalil's eyes or if she wouldn't look like me at all. I was also nervous because I didn't know anything about being a mom. It wasn't like I had a good role model for that. Luckily Khalil's mom is going to stay with us for a couple weeks once the baby gets here. I'll also have Stacey here to help me, but soon she'll have her own child to deal with as well. It's definitely going to take a village to raise this baby.

We laughed and talked for about an hour and a half before we were done and ready to go. We agreed to get together again soon but it was going to have to be at my house. I'm not going to be doing much of walking anywhere by then.

"Can I get you ladies anything else?" Claire asked as she came back to our table.

"Just a couple of carryout trays and the bill," Ryan said.

"Okay, is it all together or separate? Claire inquired.

"You can put it all together," I replied.

Claire walked away and returned a couple minutes later with the bill and containers.

Ryan reached in her purse to get her wallet but I handed the waitress my card first. Khalil had given me money to buy everybody food tonight. I told him it wasn't necessary because he had just put a hundred thousand dollars in my account a couple weeks ago.

"Oh thank you, it was going to be my treat," Ryan said.

"It's fine, this was on Khalil."

I got up to go to the bathroom while they packed up their leftover food. Once I was done and back at the table, Stacey had packed mine as well. I didn't eat a fraction of my food.

We grabbed our to-go bags and headed out of the restaurant. We looked both ways before crossing the street to the parking garage. It looked a lot darker than it was when we first got here. I was regretting not having my mace with me.

As we made it to my car, there was a man standing by it that looked like he was on drugs.

"Aye, you got ten dollars?" the man asked.

I was shocked as hell because since when has it gone from asking for change or a dollar to ten dollars?

"No, sorry, I don't have any cash with me," I answered while Stacey shook her head no.

"Bitch, you lying. I can tell you got money."

"She said she don't have any money, so keep it moving," Stacey told him.

I hit the lock on my car and as I was getting in, I got knocked off my feet from behind. I instantly put my hand out first, trying not to fall on my stomach. The first thing that came to mind was the day Khalil had me kidnapped. I knew he wasn't behind this though, because he wouldn't put me and his baby's life in jeopardy like that.

I could barely move, but I made sure to curl up in a fetal position.

"What the fuck," Stacey gasped, running over to my side of the car. She started swinging on whoever it was that knocked me down.

I tried to get up and help her but I couldn't move. Out of nowhere, someone else ran up, knocking her down as well. They started kicking her in her stomach and face. Tears instantly started falling from my eyes. I was feeling helpless watching my sister get attacked in front of me.

Once Stacey stopped moving, they focused their attention back on me. One of them kicked me in my side hard as hell, making me double over on my back while the other one kneeled over me with a knife.

"Aye, what are y'all doing?" someone yelled, coming our way.

The person lifted the knife and slashed me across my stomach. My last thought was I hope my daughter makes it if I don't, before I lost consciousness.

To be continued....

ALSO BY KEVINA HOPKINS

It's Givin' Rich Thug Energy

Addicted To A Rich Hitta 3

Addicted To A Rich Hitta 2

Addicted To A Rich Hitta

When The Side B*tch Understands The Assignment 2

Movin' Different 4: A Hood Millionaire Romance

Movin' Different 3: A Hood Millionaire Romance

Movin' Different 2: A Hood Millionaire Romance

Movin' Different: A Hood Millionaire Romance

A Chi-Town Millionaire Stole My Heart

A Chi-Town Millionaire Stole My Heart 2

A Chi-Town Millionaire Stole My Heart 3

King & Armani

King & Armani 2

King & Armani 3

I'm Just Doin' Me

I'm Just Doin' Me 2

Lil Mama A Ryder

Lil Mama A Ryder 2

When A Savage Loves A Woman

When A Savage Loves A Woman 2

The Autobiography Of A Capo's Wife

Every Dope Boy Got A Side Chick

Printed in the USA
CPSIA information can be obtained
at www.ICGtesting.com
LVHW042324180823
755636LV00002B/187

9 798393 712549